W9-AFV-751

EMMY
AND THE
INCREDIBLE
SHRINKING RAT

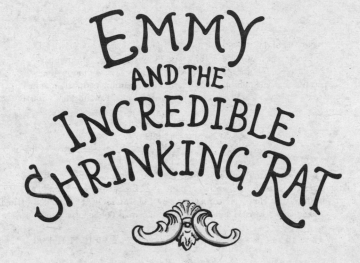

EMMY AND THE INCREDIBLE SHRINKING RAT

LYNNE JONELL

ART BY JONATHAN BEAN

SCHOLASTIC INC.
New York Toronto London Auckland Sydney
Mexico City New Delhi Hong Kong Buenos Aires

No part of this publication may be reproduced, stored in a retrieval
system, or transmitted in any form or by any means, electronic,
mechanical, photocopying, recording, or otherwise, without written
permission of the publisher. For information regarding permission, write
to Henry Holt and Company, LLC, 175 Fifth Avenue, New York, NY 10010.

ISBN-13: 978-0-545-09937-0
ISBN-10: 0-545-09937-4

Text copyright © 2007 by Lynne Jonell.
Illustrations copyright © 2007 by Jonathan Bean.
All rights reserved. Published by Scholastic Inc., 557 Broadway, New York, NY 10012,
by arrangement with Henry Holt and Company, LLC. SCHOLASTIC and associated
logos are trademarks and/or registered trademarks of Scholastic Inc.

12 11 10 9 8 7 6 5 4 3 2 1   8 9 10 11 12 13/0

Printed in the U.S.A.   40

First Scholastic printing, October 2008

Book designed by Amelia May Anderson

To my dear sister Boni,
who listened to my very first stories
and asked for more
—L. J.

EMMY WAS A GOOD GIRL. At least she tried very hard to be good.

She did her homework without being told. She ate all her vegetables, even the slimy ones. And she never talked back to her nanny, Miss Barmy, although it was almost impossible to keep quiet, some days.

Of course no one can keep this kind of thing up forever. But Miss Barmy had told Emmy that if she were a good girl, her parents would probably want to see her more often; and so Emmy kept on bravely trying.

So far it hadn't helped. Emmy's parents went on one vacation after another—to Paris, to Salamanca, to the Isle of Bugaloo—and hardly ever seemed to come home, or even to miss her at all.

"If you did better in school, I'm sure they would be pleased," said Miss Barmy, admiring her polished fingernails.

This was unjust. "My last report card was all A's," Emmy said sturdily, remembering how hard she had worked for them.

"But not a single A+, dear." Miss Barmy smiled sweetly, checking her lipstick in a pocket mirror. "And how are your ballet lessons coming? Are you getting any less clumsy?"

Emmy's shoulders slumped. She had tripped just last week.

"Really, Emmaline, your parents might pay attention to you, if you ever did anything worth paying attention *to*. Why don't you bring home some more ribbons and trophies?"

"I have a whole shelfful," Emmy said faintly.

"You'll just have to try a little harder, dear. Fill *two* shelves."

So Emmy did. Not that anyone noticed.

Still, Miss Barmy said that good girls didn't care too much about being noticed—so Emmy tried not to care.

She really was a little *too* good.

Which is why she liked to sit by the Rat.

The Rat was not good at all.

When the children at Grayson Lake Elementary reached in to feed him, he snapped at their fingers. When they had a little trouble with fractions, he sneered. And he often made cutting remarks in a low voice when the teacher was just out of earshot.

Emmy was the only one who heard him. And even she wondered sometimes if she was just imagining things.

One Wednesday in May, when not one person had seemed to notice her all morning, Emmy asked to stay indoors for recess. "I have spelling to study," she explained to Mr. Herbifore.

The teacher, hurrying out after his class, didn't look at her as he nodded permission. At least Emmy *thought* he had nodded.

"Thank you," said Emmy. And then she heard something that sounded oddly like a snort.

She looked at the Rat, and he snorted again. He was scowling, as usual.

"Why are you always so mean?" Emmy wondered aloud.

She didn't expect the Rat to answer. She'd tried to speak to him before, and he had always pretended not to hear.

But this time he curled his upper lip. "Why are *you* always so *good?*"

Emmy was too startled to respond.

The Rat shrugged one furry shoulder. "It doesn't get you anywhere. Just look at you—missing recess to study words you could spell in your sleep—and the only thing that happens is, you get ignored."

Emmy looked away. It was true.

Her parents never answered the letters she sent, even though she copied them over for neatness and gave them to Miss Barmy to mail.

Her teacher kept forgetting her name, even though she had made a placard for her desk that said EMMY in big red letters edged with silver glitter.

And she didn't want to tell the Rat, but she didn't mind missing recess at all. For Emmy, recess was a time when she felt more alone than ever.

"The bad ones get all the attention," said the Rat. "Try being bad for once. You might like it."

Emmy thought about being bad. It had its appeal.

If she were bad, she could stick out her tongue at Miss Barmy. She could call her parents long distance whenever she wanted. She could climb on her desk in school and scream until the other kids *had* to notice her . . .

"No one will like me if I'm bad," she said.

"No one likes you anyway," said the Rat bluntly.

Emmy frowned. "Well, they don't *dis*like me."

"That's right," the Rat answered promptly. "Nobody likes you, nobody dislikes you, nobody cares about you either way. You're a big nothing, if you ask me."

"I didn't," said Emmy with some spirit.

The Rat's whiskers twitched. "That's the first time I've heard you sound like anything but a piece of wet bread. Why don't you stand up for yourself more often?"

"Listen," Emmy said, "it's not like I don't *try*—"

"Yesterday, when that girl with the ponytail butted in line, you let her. And when that kid who sits across from you, the soccer star, the freckled one with hair that looks like a haystack—"

"Joe Benson."

"Yeah, him. Well, when Haystack Hair was walking backward and stepped on your foot, *you* said 'Sorry.'"

"I was just being nice," said Emmy, stung.

"You're *too* nice," said the Rat sharply. "A little meanness is good for the soul. I highly recommend it."

Emmy lifted her chin. "Being mean doesn't get *you* anywhere. Nobody pets you. Nobody plays with you."

"I get what I want," said the Rat, showing his long, yellow teeth. "I get respect, which is more than I can say for you."

Emmy glared at him. "*You* get respect? You live in a *cage*."

The Rat looked stunned.

"Well, it's true," Emmy said crossly. "Don't tell me you haven't noticed. You know, the bars, the lock on the door . . ."

The Rat's whiskers trembled. "You're not being very nice."

"Nice? I thought a little meanness was good for the—"

"Most people don't mention it. Most people know better than to taunt a rodent about his . . . unfortunate situation."

"Look, *you* were the one who said—"

"It's not *my* fault I'm locked up!" The Rat's voice quavered pathetically. "I committed no crime! Have I

survived kidnapping from the nest, unjust imprison-
ment, and absolutely appalling food"—he gave his
dish of pellets a contemptuous kick—"only to be
mocked by a little child?"

"I'm bigger than you," Emmy began hotly, "and
you were the one who said I shouldn't be so nice—"

"But not to me! It's different when you're mean
to *me*!"

"Oh, right," said Emmy.

There was a thunder of footsteps and a clatter of
voices in the hall. Emmy watched resignedly as her
classmates poured in, laughing and talking. They all
seemed friendly enough—to one another—but no
matter how Emmy tried, they just looked right
through her as though she weren't there.

Why were things so different here? At her old
school, she had had lots of friends. But then her parents had inherited all that money and moved across
town to live in Great-Great-Uncle William's old mansion on the shores of Grayson Lake, and after that a
lot of things had changed.

Maybe it's me, Emmy thought dismally. Maybe
I've turned into some horrible person and I don't
even know it.

She opened a book and bent her head, letting her straight brown hair fall around her face like a curtain. But as the children around her quieted down, she heard a small sob.

Emmy peeked sideways. The Rat had retreated to the far corner of his cage, his face buried in his forepaws. He looked as if he were sleeping. But Emmy saw the Rat's gray shoulders heave, and after a while one small paw emerged to wipe the corner of his eye.

Poor Rat. For all his tough talk, he was awfully sensitive. Apparently she shouldn't have mentioned his cage.

"Sorry," she whispered. And then the phone on the teacher's desk rang.

"Emma? Emmaline Addison?" Mr. Herbifore gazed out over the heads of his students.

Emmy stood up.

"No, I don't see her," he said into the phone.

Joe Benson snickered.

Emmy walked forward and stood by the teacher's desk. What did she have to do, she wondered, bewildered. Throw firecrackers under his chair? Hang from the ceiling and make like a monkey?

She tugged at the teacher's sleeve and spoke loudly in his ear. "Here I am, Mr. Herbifore."

The teacher stared at her doubtfully. "Oh? Are you sure?" He looked puzzled. "Well, you're wanted in Dr. Leander's office."

Emmy knocked grumpily at Dr. Leander's door. She *hated* visiting the psychologist. She already had to sit there an hour every other week, just making up stuff for him to write in his blue notebook; why did she have to go *again*?

The door opened. Emmy stepped back.

"Hello, dear," said Miss Barmy.

The nanny had soft dark hair and green eyes, rimmed with gold like a cat's. Her lipstick was a slick pink, and when she smiled she showed a glimpse of perfectly even teeth, like a row of white chisels.

Dr. Leander was gazing at her with open admiration. Men always did admire Miss Barmy; Emmy didn't know why.

Maybe it was the odd cane she carried that everyone found so fascinating. Or maybe men thought she was pretty. Years ago, Emmy knew, Miss Barmy had won a beauty contest. But in spite of that, Emmy thought the nanny's face looked hard, as if all the makeup were a polished pink shell that no one could crack.

"Now then, Emmaline, Dr. Leander has kindly offered us the use of his conference room."

The psychologist opened a side door with a grand gesture.

Emmy sat down stiffly. "Have I done something wrong?"

Miss Barmy brushed a fleck from her linen cuff. "Well, you *did* contradict me this morning about the time of your parents' arrival."

Emmy frowned. Her parents' plane was supposed to land tomorrow evening at five thirty, she had been sure. But Miss Barmy had insisted the correct time was an hour later.

And this was so important that she had to miss class?

Don't, Emmy thought fiercely, *don't* tell me I can't meet them at the airport.

Miss Barmy smiled. "Never fear—you can still drive with Jems to the airport. I know how precious are the tender bonds between parent and child . . ."

How did Miss Barmy manage to guess Emmy's thoughts so often? It was creepy.

". . . yet when you contradict me, clearly something is not in balance. Perhaps the vitamin cell repositories . . . or the beta-hydroxy of the brain. You could even be having an epidermal skin sensitivity . . ."

Emmy flinched. The last time Miss Barmy had identified a skin problem, she had given Emmy a special tonic to cleanse her inner system. Unfortunately, it had turned her face a vivid orange for a whole week.

Another time, Miss Barmy had taken Emmy off sugar for months, saying she was trying to discover if Emmy's behavior problems were allergy related. Emmy had almost cried on her tenth birthday, when everyone else was given an exceptionally large slice of five-layer chocolate cake—and she got a tofu bar.

". . . but the herbology inoculum is, I think, the best solution, and I trust you'll soon feel the corrective effect of the proper reflexology balance. There, Emmaline, drink it all, and you'll feel ever so much better."

Emmy looked with distaste at the bottle of Spring Peach Essence to which Miss Barmy had added three drops from a small, unlabeled vial. The liquid turned from pale pink to swirling violet and emitted a faint puff of vapor.

"Quickly, now, before the vitamin distillate is absorbed by the ozone!" Miss Barmy spoke sharply. "Or I will keep you in your room when your parents come!"

Emmy shut her eyes, held her nose, and gulped the liquid down. She *had* to see her parents first thing. They had been gone for weeks, and the ride home from the airport was always the best. Snuggled between her mom and dad in the back seat, laughing and talking, it was almost like the old days, before they had moved from the apartment above their bookstore—before Miss Barmy.

Miss Barmy dropped the vial into her square lizard-skin purse and closed the jaws with a snap. Dr. Leander stood hastily as she opened the door.

"Thank you ever so much," Miss Barmy said sweetly. "Emmaline forgot to take her medicine, and I had to give a corrective dose."

"Of course," said Dr. Leander, holding on to Miss

Barmy's hand longer than was strictly necessary. "Please call on me anytime, anytime at all."

Emmy trudged back to her classroom, hoping that her face hadn't turned blue, or pimply, or that her hair hadn't started to fall out. Why did Miss Barmy keep giving her medicine? She was never sick. And she didn't have mental problems, so why did the nanny keep setting up appointments with the psychologist?

"*I'm* not the one who's crazy," Emmy muttered to the Rat as she sat down.

But the Rat was still sulking and wouldn't look at her. So Emmy wrote a note, rolled it up tight, and pushed it between the bars of the Rat's cage just as the bell rang. She didn't bother to make sure no one was watching her, because no one ever did.

"Hey, Emmy," whispered Joe Benson, grinning all over his freckled face, "are you sure that rat can read?"

2

EMMY STARED AT JOE. Someone had spoken to her! Someone actually knew her name!

"Um . . . ," she said, stalling for time. How could she explain writing a note to a *rodent*?

Joe leaned over her desk. "Just watch out for his teeth," he advised, showing a bandaged finger. "He bit me yesterday after school."

"Really?" said Emmy, still amazed to be having an actual conversation. "How come?"

"*I* don't know. I was just trying to feed him a carrot. You'd think he would have been grateful."

"Ha!" said the Rat indignantly.

Joe's head swiveled slowly to face the cage on the window ledge. His mouth opened. No sound came out.

"How would *you* like it," the Rat went on, folding his paws over his chest, "if someone tried to mash a gigantic carrot into *your* mouth?"

Joe looked back at Emmy. "Did you just hear—" He faltered, glancing uneasily at the Rat.

All around them, the classroom was noisy with banging desktops and shuffling feet. No one else showed any interest in the Rat as he picked up Emmy's note.

Joe was suddenly surrounded by his friends.

"Hurry up, Joe!"

"We'll have to run laps if we're late to soccer again."

"What's the matter, you slowing down?"

Emmy gathered her books, unnoticed by all except Joe, who stared at her wildly.

She grinned at him through the jostling heads and shoulders, and then she was swept into the stream of children that poured from the classroom, through the hall, and out the big double doors that led to the playground.

The sun was bright and warm, and Emmy still had a little time before her ballet class. She slipped quickly between a hedge of bushes and the rough brick of the schoolhouse wall and squatted there to catch her breath.

The big lilacs screened her from everyone in the schoolyard. It was a perfect spot to hide, or just to sit and think. Emmy had sat there sometimes during recess, making little faces in the leaves with her fingernail. It was sort of dopey, but it was better than trying to join a game and getting ignored, or talking to people who walked right past her.

But Joe had talked to her today. And he had heard the Rat, too. Why was that? Emmy wondered, crawling along the narrow space between the brick wall and the bushes.

One, two, three . . . She counted windows as she passed. There was Mr. Herbifore's desk. Four, five . . . She lifted her head cautiously and looked through the window directly into the Rat's cage. He had picked up her note and spread it against the wall of his cage, bracing it with his paws. And even though the bottom corner kept curling up, Emmy could read the note from where she crouched. It said:

> *I'm sorry I was mean. It didn't*
> *feel as good as you said it would.*
> > *Emmy*
> *P.S. Is respect ALL you want?*

The Rat's mouth moved silently as he read the words. He was so close that Emmy could see a small patch of white fur just behind his left ear. She cleared her throat.

The Rat whirled around, glared, and instantly turned his back.

Leaves tickled Emmy's neck, and the sun warmed her hands where they pressed against the windowsill. "It's dumb," she said at last, "to pretend I'm not here."

The Rat tapped one foot lightly, saying nothing.

"It's not only dumb, it's mean."

The Rat made an indistinct noise that sounded like "Huh!"

"It's the meanest thing in the world," said Emmy severely, "to ignore someone. It makes a person feel like she doesn't even exist."

The Rat lifted his nose. "I'll tell you what's mean," he said to the air. "It's when certain people taunt imprisoned rodents about their . . . substandard housing. And it's even worse," he went on, his voice rising, "when I have to watch *that!*" He pointed over Emmy's right shoulder.

Emmy peered around the lilac bush. There was nothing much to see. Joe and his friends were on the soccer field, kicking a ball around. Beyond, through the trees, Emmy could see the storefronts of Main Street and the little studio where she took ballet every Wednesday afternoon. Farther down the hill to the left, she could just see the third story of her house, and its red-tiled roof, and her bedroom window. And after that was nothing but lake and sky.

She looked back through the window at the Rat. "Watch what?" she asked curiously.

The Rat waved his paw irritably at the soccer fields. A distant ball rose in a perfect arc, white and black against the greening trees, and a faint sound of cheering drifted across the grass. "I could do that," the Rat muttered.

"What? Kick a goal?"

"Be a star." The Rat gripped the bars of his cage. "I've practiced in my cage. Other rodents—they play, out there, in the moonlight. They try, but . . ." The Rat drew himself up to his full height. "I'd show them how it's done. They'd be astonished. They'd elect me captain—"

"Rodents play soccer?" Emmy asked, incredulous.

The Rat scowled. "Of course they play soccer," he snapped. "What do you *think* they do for fun? Run about, frightening elephants? Scavenge in churches for crumbs? Really, your ignorance is appalling. Modern rodents have *many* and *varied* interests."

"I—didn't know," Emmy stammered. "I'm sor—"

"And don't apologize! You do that *all* the time!"

Emmy frowned.

The Rat sighed. "Shouldn't you be getting home? Won't your parents be worried?"

"They're out of town." Emmy shrugged. "Anyway, Wednesdays I have ballet after school, and then French, so nobody's expecting me yet." She stared out past the trees and toward the lake, and pointed. "There's my house."

The Rat squinted. "What? That castle-looking thing?"

"It does look a little like a castle," Emmy admitted. "My bedroom's in that top turret—with the blue window."

The Rat looked at her thoughtfully. "It's a lot bigger than the other houses."

"Thirty-three rooms," said Emmy gloomily, "nine bathrooms, a housekeeper, a gardener, and a chauffeur. Oh, and Miss Barmy, my nanny."

"What?" the Rat said again. "No parents?"

"I told you, they're out of town. They've been gone for five weeks and three days, but they're coming back tomorrow night." She looked at her watch, squinting in the bright sun. "I really should get going."

But the Rat's attention was back on the soccer field, where Joe had just scored another goal. The Rat leaned forward until his nose was poking through the bars of his cage, his whole body tense with yearning.

Emmy, watching, felt something come over her. It was a feeling—unusual for her—that she very much wanted to do something she wasn't supposed to do. Her hand drifted up through the open window . . . her fingers found the latch of the cage. . . .

She hesitated. If anyone saw her, Miss Barmy might find out. If Miss Barmy found out, she would give Emmy's parents a bad report—and then they might not come home at all.

There was a stifled moan from the Rat. His gaze was riveted to the latch, and his whole body was trembling. Then, as Emmy watched, he clasped his paws together in front of his chest, looked beseechingly into her eyes, and dropped to his knees with a little thump.

Emmy wavered for a heartbeat—and lifted the latch.

The Rat knelt, perfectly still, for one incredulous moment. And then he leaped to his feet. "I'm free! I'm free!" he shrieked, hopping up and down. He scrambled to the windowsill and launched himself into the air, landing with a puff of dust.

In an instant he was running, scampering, rolling through the wide grassy schoolyard like a small gray juggernaut. "Freeeeeee!" came a last high, thin cry, faint in the open air, and then he was gone.

Emmy walked across the schoolyard, her shoes scuffing at the grass. The thought occurred to her that Miss Barmy would want her to pick up her feet. She didn't do it.

Of course she hadn't expected the Rat to say thank you. He had never been a polite sort of rodent. But for him to leave so suddenly, without even a goodbye, gave Emmy a hollow feeling.

The Rat had been someone to talk to, even if he *was* rude. Now all she had to look forward to was the same old class, with the same old kids who never seemed to know she was alive.

Well, no, that wasn't quite true anymore. Emmy passed the soccer field and brightened as she saw Joe, who was standing with his father. She walked slowly past them, listening in spite of herself.

"And I've told you before, Son—if they try a wall pass, you have to follow the player, not the ball. Now don't let them fool you again."

Emmy wondered for a moment what it would be like to have the kind of father who would come to her activities, put his hand on her shoulder, and give her friendly advice.

But Joe wasn't listening. He seemed to be gazing off in the distance.

Had the Rat run that way? Emmy walked on toward the trees that bordered the playfield—and stopped. A small gray animal bounded through the grass and leaped to a tree trunk. It balanced itself with its long, bushy tail.

Emmy sighed. It was only a squirrel. Another came right after the first, darting through the under-brush and to the base of the tree, its claws out and digging into the bark, its long, pink tail—*pink* tail?

Emmy sharpened to attention as the Rat scrabbled up the tree. He climbed fairly well, especially considering how long he had lived in a cage with only a wire wheel that went round and round.

The Rat caught up to the squirrel at the first fork in the trunk and began to speak, waving a paw in the air as if to emphasize a point. Emmy couldn't make out his words, but as far as she could tell, the Rat seemed to be introducing himself. The squirrel's mouth dropped open.

The Rat talked a little louder. Emmy caught a few words now—"pellets" and "appalling" and "lunch."

The squirrel looked distinctly dimwitted. The Rat gave an irritated snort. And then, with a sudden flurry, the squirrel leaped past the Rat, flew up three branches, and disappeared into a knothole.

The Rat's mouth fell open in ludicrous imitation of the squirrel.

Emmy stifled a laugh.

The Rat's jaw snapped shut. "And just what, may I ask, is so funny?"

"Oh—nothing." Emmy tried for a serious tone. "Are you enjoying your freedom?"

The Rat gave a loud and disapproving sniff. "I might enjoy it more if certain people weren't here." He looked sternly at Emmy. "Some rodents are shy of humans. Understandably, I might add, given your long and bloody history."

"Long and *bloody*?"

"Even your nursery rhymes—need I remind you of 'Three Blind Mice'? Hardly fit for children, I *must* say."

"But that's just a—"

The Rat interrupted coldly. "It's too bad I can't have a little chat with a friend without you showing up to scare him off."

"*Me?*" Emmy was annoyed. "It was *you*—"

"I *beg* your pardon." The sarcasm was very apparent. "I shall resume the conversation which was so *rudely* interrupted. Kindly do not interfere."

Emmy was speechless. She watched as the Rat climbed majestically up the trunk, pausing now and then to shake a hind foot as if to ward off a cramp. He arrived at the entrance to the squirrel's home, adjusted his neck fur, and knocked.

There was a sudden wild flurry of gray fur at the knothole. One paw swiped out, claws extended.

The Rat backed down. "I say," he called, sounding aggrieved, "you could hurt someone like that!"

The squirrel's head poked out of the hole. His furry arm held the stem of a very large acorn.

"I don't really care for nuts, thank you," the Rat began. And then, with one swift movement, the acorn was flung with startling accuracy at the Rat's head.

It landed with a crack. The Rat gave a yelp and tumbled down, somersaulting, his little pink feet flailing helplessly in the air. And then Emmy caught him.

He lay cradled between her palms, limp and gasping for breath. His small, plump body was surprisingly soft in her hands. She could see the patch of white fur behind his left ear—such an even triangular shape—and a thin trail of moisture from his quivering nose. Suddenly she felt full of pity for this small, arrogant, impossible creature, and she stroked the back of his head gently with her thumb.

The Rat opened his eyes. "Kindly do not *pet* me. My name is not Fido, nor is it Fluffy. Put me down at once."

Emmy set the Rat down gently in the grass. He struggled to sit up, looking very stiff.

"You have been of some service to me," he said frostily. "But let's get one thing straight. I have my own life to live, and I *don't* want you following me.

Your mere presence drove that poor squirrel mad, and he"—the Rat sniffed—"he was just about to invite me to lunch."

Emmy looked at him. "You honestly think that squirrel—"

The Rat waved an airy paw. "I accept your apology. Now leave me alone."

"I'm *not* apologizing, you nutcase—"

"Go *away*! Leave me *alone*! Get a *life*!"

Emmy stared at the imperious Rat, and turned on her heel. "Fine," she said bitterly. "I'm going."

She crossed Main Street without looking for cars. She heard the screech of brakes behind her as she reached the art gallery, ran past the alley with its overflowing trash cans, and up the worn wooden steps that led to the ballet studio.

She paused on the landing, catching her breath. That ungrateful Rat. *Now* she knew why rats had such a bad reputation.

She glared through the half-open door to the dance studio. The smell of stale socks assailed her nose as a dozen sweaty little girls in leotards leaped awkwardly. And suddenly Emmy couldn't stand the thought of pulling on a leotard and sweating with them.

She gazed crossly into the alley below. She wouldn't go to dance class. She wouldn't go. What was the use of trying to do everything she was supposed to when nobody ever cared anyway?

Emmy was flooded with a fierce excitement. She pelted down the sagging stairs and skidded onto the sidewalk. She looked up and down the street—at all the shops she had visited with Miss Barmy—and then she caught sight of the alley again. It stretched out before her, dark and messy and forbidding.

She hesitated. It looked dirty. It looked dangerous.

She stepped in.

EMMY WALKED QUICKLY down the narrow alley, her footsteps echoing off the walls that rose on either side of her like a canyon of sooty brick. A smell of overripe fruit and spoiled meat curled up from the brimming trash cans.

But then there was light again, and a central triangle of patchy grass like a little park, and a wonderful maze of backstreets that she had never seen before, crammed with shops.

Emmy gazed around, delighted. Miss Barmy had only taken her to stores where mannequins wore expensive suits and jewelers spoke in quiet voices over glass countertops. These shops were—well—shabbier, but they looked a lot more interesting.

She wandered by a candy store, its window filled with colorful jars—peppermints, gumdrops, chocolate nibbles, all packed full of sugar, and not a tofu bar in sight! A smiling woman was handing out caramels at the door . . . they were unwrapped. They probably weren't at all sanitary. Emmy took three and popped them in her mouth all at once.

An exuberant puppy, small, white, and yappy, bounced out of a side street and went straight for Emmy's ankles, drooling. Emmy got another caramel from the lady and dropped it in the dog's mouth.

There was a tattoo parlor with foreign-looking letters on its sign and a big, hairy man getting tattooed right in the window. Emmy watched in fascination as the needle was poked into his back. She wasn't exactly sure what was being tattooed, but she was fairly certain Miss Barmy wouldn't have approved.

There was a small grocery that smelled of fish and a bakery that smelled of vanilla and almonds. A narrow building next door carried the sign HOME FOR TROUBLED GIRLS, and Emmy giggled, feeling unaccountably wild and silly. "Troubled, that's me," she said gaily to the puppy, dancing a few steps to the flamenco music blaring from the shop across the street.

No wonder Miss Barmy never came here. No expensive clothes to buy, no fashionable people to impress, and no health-food stores anywhere. There *was* a shoe store, though. Emmy looked at it doubtfully. Miss Barmy always had metal tips put on her shoes. Emmy thought that maybe she just liked to hear herself walk.

There was a white-haired man outside the shoe-shop door who was sitting on a little stool, whittling a block of wood. He was soft-looking, rather like a dumpling dressed in old clothes, and his face was wrinkled.

Emmy edged closer. A long, curly shaving peeled off his knife.

"Want to see, missy?" he asked, as the puppy pounced on the wood shaving. "Mister Bee don't mind none." The old man ran a hand through what was left of his hair and looked up at Emmy with a gentle expression.

"Who's Mr. Bee? Is he your boss?" Emmy reached out a finger, touching the small pointed face of the little carving. Was it an otter? Or maybe a—

Crash! A flowerpot, thrown from above, broke on the sidewalk.

"MIS-TER BEE! Are you *working*, or are you *jabbering*?"

The screech came from an upstairs window. Emmy looked up, startled. There was nothing to be seen but a scrawny hand pulling back the lace curtains and shaking a finger.

"Working, dear!" called the chubby old man, instantly picking up his knife again. "Working hard, as always, my little rosebud!"

There was a vigorous snort. "Then see that you keep at it, you old fool!" Another flowerpot flew past, just missing Emmy's foot.

The man leaned closer to Emmy. "*I'm* Mister Bee," he whispered, "and up there—that's my boss. Missus Bee. Here, step under the awning so she don't hit you."

He glanced up at the window, chuckling. "She's a beautiful woman, my Addie, but she's always had a bit of a temper."

Beautiful? Emmy craned her neck, but the scrawny hand, yellow as a chicken leg, was all she could see.

"Mis-ter BEE!"

Emmy dodged a violently thrown cup and saucer and fled toward the corner, where there stood a stately house of faded blue. She ducked behind a sign that read P. PEEBLES, ATTORNEY AT LAW and looked back at Mr. Bee. He was sweeping up the broken pieces as calmly as if he did it every day.

Relieved to be out of range, Emmy cut across the tip of the green to what looked like a pet shop, on the next corner. A painted sign swung from the doorway. Emmy ran closer to see, and the puppy followed, barking happily. On the sign was painted a familiar gray form, and beneath it, tall, spidery letters spelled out THE ANTIQUE RAT.

The storefront was old-fashioned–looking, with vine-covered brick and broad windowsills. Emmy pressed her nose to the smudged and dusty glass. She could make out carved tables and chairs . . . she slumped, disappointed. It was just an ordinary antique store—the kind that the housekeeper, Mrs. Brecksniff, had dragged her into more than once when Miss Barmy had her day off. There were no cages, or rats, or any pets at all.

Emmy looked down at her feet, where the excitable puppy was licking her shoe. Maybe her parents would allow her to keep the puppy if she asked them. Sometimes, when they came home from a trip, they were very loving for a while. Emmy was scratching the puppy behind the ears, considering this, when a familiar rhythm stopped her cold.

It was the sound of footsteps. Firm footsteps. Rapid, purposeful footsteps, made by shoes with metal tips, and every so often another thunking sound, out of rhythm.

The puppy whimpered, and Emmy drifted like smoke deep into the shadowed entryway. Only one person in the world sounded like that when she walked.

Fighting an inner dread, Emmy quietly turned the brass doorknob of the Antique Rat. A bell tinkled faintly in a back room, and a fine dusting of grime sifted down from the top of the frame. Emmy eased the door shut and stood behind it. She could see a bit of the street from this angle, and her breath quickened as a woman's legs came into view, along with a swinging cane. Lizard-skin shoes stopped abruptly, pointing at the storefront, and the cane came to rest. Miss Barmy was looking in the window.

Emmy flattened herself against the door. She didn't need to look at the cane to see it. Made of hardwood, polished almost white, it was intricately carved with miniature faces, their hair intertwined.

Miss Barmy said they were the faces of people she had taken care of. She'd promised that someday she would have Emmy's face carved on one of the blank patches.

Emmy suppressed a shudder. Every grown-up who ever saw the cane told Emmy she was a lucky girl to have such a remarkable nanny. But something about the little faces bothered her.

The footsteps started up again. Emmy could hear them passing the window, scraping on the step, and stopping at the door. She slid sideways, silent as a cat, and crouched behind a large and dusty dresser just as the doorknob turned.

"Yes?" said a voice: a teenage boy, Emmy guessed. She pressed her face against the side of the dresser, breathing softly. It wasn't that she was afraid of Miss Barmy—not exactly, she told herself. It would just be so much easier if she didn't have to explain skipping ballet.

All was quiet. Emmy could almost feel Miss Barmy's eyes looking the person up and down.

"May I help you?" The boy's voice was patient.

"Who are you? Where is Mr. Vole?" Miss Barmy's usually silken voice sounded abrupt.

"My uncle is out just now. Is there something I can do for you?"

The cane tapped on the floorboards. "I can't wait. I'll leave a message."

"Yes?"

"Tell your—uncle, did you say?—that I want the usual," Miss Barmy said sharply. "Tomorrow evening, ten minutes to six, on the dot."

"The . . . the usual?"

"He'll know what I mean. And I want it delivered quietly, you understand? Come to the back door and knock twice. I'll be waiting."

There was a soft sound of scratching, like a pencil on paper. "And the name?"

"He'll know who I am," Miss Barmy said coldly. "I'm the one who doesn't pay."

"D—doesn't pay?" the boy stammered. "I don't think my uncle will allow—I mean, his rates are very expensive—"

"They're *exorbitant*, young man, they're highway robbery. Fortunately, Mr. Vole and I have an agreement. Oh, he'll be very glad to let me have the usual, for no fee at all. You'll see."

"Yes, ma'am. And where should it be delivered?"

"The old Addison mansion on Grayson Lake. It's the last house on Loon's Bay Road. Don't forget—five fifty tomorrow, back door, double knock."

"Yes, ma'am."

There was a gritty sound of shoes turning, of steps, of the door creaking open.

Emmy held her breath.

"Tell your uncle to see to it personally," Miss Barmy said, "or I shall be *seriously* disturbed."

Emmy poked her head out as the footsteps died away.

The boy was tall and slightly pudgy, with stooped shoulders and a pale complexion. His ears stuck out from hair that needed a trim, but he looked at her kindly.

Emmy felt awkward. Should she apologize for listening in and hearing Miss Barmy order—what *had* she ordered, anyway? She glanced out the window in time to see Miss Barmy disappear into the shoe shop across the street.

Emmy shut her eyes. She had had a narrow escape.

"Feeling kind of shaky?" The boy's hand on her elbow was warm. "Here, sit down. It's the rats, you know."

"The . . . the rats?" Emmy sat obediently on a green velvet chair embroidered with small white creatures.

"They make some people queasy." The boy waved his hand at the cluttered interior of the shop. "My uncle's got rats on the brain."

Emmy followed the boy's gaze. The shop was packed with furniture of all kinds—small round tables, straight-backed chairs, great gilded mirrors—and on every piece there was painted or carved or embroidered some kind of rodent for decoration.

"Do people actually—" Emmy paused, feeling that the question she wanted to ask was not quite polite.

"Buy this stuff?" The boy grinned and shifted his broom. "Not much. But sometimes people come for the real ones."

"Your uncle sells rats?" Emmy was struck by a thought. "Does he catch them himself?" She waited for the answer, thinking worriedly of Rat, *her* rat. He was rude and ungrateful, but he was still her friend. Emmy didn't think she could bear to see him caged again.

The boy shrugged. "I don't know," he admitted.

"But my uncle doesn't collect ordinary rats, and the people who come here don't want ordinary rats."

He laughed, tucking a notebook and pencil into his back pocket. "I wouldn't even say that the people who come here are ordinary people. A little weird, most of them."

Emmy nodded. Miss Barmy was weird enough. What had she been doing in a rat shop, and what was it she wanted delivered to Emmy's house tomorrow evening at ten minutes to six?

Emmy passed a hand over her forehead. Ballet probably wasn't over yet. If she ran, she could make some excuse about why she was late. If she turned around and walked out right now, she could be through the dark alley and back in her safe and ordinary world in two minutes flat.

The boy peered at her. "You still look kind of squeamish. Rats are okay, once you get to know them. Better than people, sometimes." His smile became a bit uncertain. "Want something to drink?"

Emmy nodded.

The boy led the way to an alcove in the rear of the store with a lumpy maroon couch. "Have a seat. I'll be right back." He opened a door behind the couch and clumped up a set of long, narrow stairs.

There were books stacked on the couch with titles like *My Life Among the Rats: A Memoir* and *Scientific Rodentology 101*. Emmy was paging through one called *Lemmings or Leaders?* when she heard a rustling sort of noise. Instinctively, she pulled up her feet and looked under the couch.

There it was again! Something *had* rustled, behind that doorway hung with a red velvet curtain.

The boy tromped down the stairs. "Here." He held out a glass of something fizzy. "My name's Brian. What's yours?"

"Emmy." She took a sip and smiled at Brian. He was the homeliest teenager she had ever seen, but also— in an odd way—the nicest looking. He smiled back.

"Do you want to see the rats? You won't be able to buy any—nobody buys them, they only rent them anyway—"

"You *rent* rats?"

"Uncle says they're so rare, nobody can afford them. But it doesn't cost anything to look."

Emmy thought Brian might be surprised at what

she could afford, but she followed him through the doorway hung with red velvet. A slight animal odor made her nose wrinkle, and she stepped inside with a feeling that she was entering another world. The faint noises from the street were suddenly muffled as the heavy velvet dropped behind her, and in the silence she could hear a rustling as every animal in the cages—or so it seemed—turned to face her. She held back a gasp as a large rodent with bright orange teeth lifted its head.

"Don't worry, that's just the beaver." Brian patted the top of the cage. "She's big but she's gentle. Aren't you, girl?"

A bell tinkled lightly. "I'll be right back," Brian said, brushing through the velvet curtain.

Was a beaver a rat? Perhaps a sort of cousin.

The beaver gazed at her through tired-looking eyes. "Poor thing," said Emmy, moving on.

Cage after cage held some kind of rodent, from the Giant Rat of Sumatra to the tiniest vole, each with its own label, and most seemed irritable, or worse. Emmy was beginning to wonder if the Rat had been a particularly good-tempered specimen after all when she caught sight of a very small mouse with big ears and huge, dark eyes. It looked appealingly at her and touched one small paw to the bars of its cage.

Emmy squatted on her heels, peering in. What a tiny little thing, and so pretty! Its fawn-colored fur looked as soft and light as dandelion fuzz. Longing to hold it in her hand, Emmy ignored all the warnings Miss Barmy had ever given against touching strange animals and put one finger between the bars.

The little mouse curled its tail up tight. It looked at Emmy, its enormous brown eyes thoughtful. And then it reached out a paw and patted Emmy's finger exactly three times in quick succession.

It clasped its paws immediately behind its back as if waiting for her to make the next move, and Emmy sucked in her breath. It was too much to believe that she should find another rodent as exceptional as the Rat. But— "Can you speak?" she whispered.

The mouse looked at her attentively but said nothing. Emmy lifted the tag that was attached to the cage. "Endear Mouse," she read aloud.

Emmy had heard of deer mice before, but never an *endear* mouse. "Must be a misprint," she decided, turning the tag over. And there, on the other side, in very small type, she read: "Endear Mouse. Makes the absent heart grow fonder. Use as directed. Satisfaction guaranteed."

"Makes the absent heart grow fonder," Emmy whispered. "Do you really?"

The tiny mouse looked at her for a long moment. Then it placed its two front paws over its chest and bowed very low.

"Do you—" Emmy paused, swallowing painfully. "I mean, can you do it for *two* absent hearts? Grown-up ones?"

The mouse looked searchingly at Emmy with its dark, beautiful eyes. And then it smiled ever so slowly and gently. It nodded twice.

Desire flooded Emmy's heart and brain. If only, if only . . . could she somehow buy this mouse? How much *was* it? For the first time ever, she felt glad to be rich. She had a room full of expensive toys that she hardly used. Could she sell those? Emmy whirled to her feet, unable to sit still, and began to pace.

She looked at the other cages. What other wonderful things could these rats do? She turned over tag after tag, reading. "Infusion of courage." "Guaranteed to sniff out a lie." "To induce calming sleep." "Makes the fat become thin." "Triples maturity." "Grows thick hair fast."

Emmy's eyes wandered from cage to cage. No wonder these rodents were expensive. People would pay almost anything to have some of these things; and there were more that she hadn't even read yet. Emmy reached for the next tag—and stopped with her hand in midair.

The animal slumped in the cage was an ordinary gray rat, the size of a squirrel. But on the back of its head, visible just behind the ear, was a triangular patch of white fur.

"RAT!" GASPED EMMY.

The rodent ignored her.

"Listen"—Emmy gripped the cage, frantic to get the animal's attention—"I'll get you out, no matter what it costs."

There was a sound of footsteps behind her, and a swish of the velvet curtain. "Brian!" cried Emmy, without turning around. "How much is this rat?"

"More than you have in your piggy bank," rasped an unfamiliar voice. "Get your fingers away from that cage! If you're bitten, you'll be sorry!"

Emmy turned her head. Brian was hovering apologetically in the background. In front of him stood what could only be the uncle.

Shorter than his nephew, he looked like someone who had shrunk while his clothes hadn't. His trousers were loose and belted high, his shirt was at least two sizes too big, and he exuded the musty smell of a closet that hadn't been aired for years.

"Emmy, this is my uncle, Professor Vole."

A professor? thought Emmy, incredulous. A professor of what? Rats?

"Nice to meet you," she said, lifting her chin. "But I don't use piggy banks. I prefer blue chip stocks." Not for nothing had she listened in on conversations about her parents' investments.

"Well." Professor Vole placed his fingertips together. "In any case, that *particular* rat is not for sale. Look at the tag, little girl."

Emmy lifted the tag, irritated. She was almost eleven: hardly a little girl anymore. "Shrinking Rat of Schenectady," she read aloud, and turned it over. "Sold in pairs only."

Emmy frowned. The Rat was still hunched over, unmoving. What had this—this rat man done to him? Just a short time ago he had been as sassy and full of himself as always, and now . . .

"That's *my* rat," she said firmly. "You must have just caught him. I saw him somewhere else only an hour ago."

Professor Vole blinked. "You saw another rat, you say?"

"No, *this* one. I'd know him anywhere."

The man tapped his fingertips together one after the other, looking thoughtful. "Brian," he said, "how long have you cared for this particular rat?"

"Ever since you brought me here to work. Almost a whole month." Brian smiled his kind smile. "So it can't be yours after all, Emmy."

Emmy looked at Brian. His face was transparently honest; it was impossible to imagine him telling a lie.

"Maybe—" She paused. "Could it be another rat that looks like him?"

"Yes." Professor Vole's fingers interlocked. "And where, exactly, did you see this other rat?" His voice was carefully casual, but behind his gold-rimmed spectacles, his eyes glinted.

"Oh, around," said Emmy uneasily. "But—"

"But what, my dear?" Professor Vole reached out a bony hand, his thin lips stretched in an attempt at a smile. "Brian, get our guest another soda."

Brian backed out, looking worried.

"But how can there be two rats with the exact same patch of white fur behind the ear— Hey! That hurts!"

The bony fingers clutched her arm. The rat man bent until his face was almost touching hers. Emmy could see the dark pores on the end of his beaky nose and short hairs like bristles poking out from his nostrils.

"What did you say?" His voice was fierce.

"I said, 'That hurts!'" Emmy tried to pull her arm away, but his grip was unrelenting.

"No, before that. What were you saying about *two* rats?" The man squeezed a little harder.

"I said it was odd to have two rats the same—"

"And the white patch behind the ear?"

"Yes!" Emmy gasped. "Just the same—"

"What was the shape?" he demanded, his breath smelling like stale crackers. "A circle? A square?"

"No—a triangle—*please* let me go, I haven't done anything—"

With a grip like iron, the professor turned Emmy to face the cage. "There!" he said, his voice reedy with excitement. "Think! Was your rat's white patch behind the right ear, like this one, or the left?"

Emmy looked, trembling. The white patch was certainly behind the right ear on the rat in the cage. But how could this awful man expect her to remember which ear it was behind on *her* rat? And how in the world was she supposed to think when she was terrified?

47

But any idea she had about asking him these questions was quickly rejected at the sight of his face. His watery blue eyes were popping with red veins, the sinews on his neck stood out like waxed rope, and altogether he had such a look of deranged lunacy that Emmy shut her eyes.

Think, think. When had she last noticed the Rat's white patch? He had been up in the tree . . . the squirrel had thrown a nut . . . he had fallen down, down, into her hands. . . .

Emmy concentrated. She had held the Rat. She had stroked the white patch. She remembered how the fur disappeared under her thumb and then sprang back into place. . . .

She opened her eyes. "It was the *left* ear!" She laughed in relief. "You were right, this one isn't my rat. I'm so sorry."

The rat man's stained teeth showed in an elated grin, and he clapped his hands together.

Completely mental, Emmy thought, backing up. She lifted the velvet curtain—

"Where is this rat?" The professor moved to block her way. "I'll pay any price you ask!"

"He's . . . not mine," Emmy stammered. "He's the classroom pet."

"What class? What school?" The man's voice shook. "Has he bitten anyone? Is he locked up?"

Emmy couldn't admit that she'd let the Rat go—this demented man was capable of anything. "He was still in his cage when I left class today," she said truthfully, sliding her feet another few inches. She ducked behind the curtain.

"Here you go, Emmy. Want a root beer?"

Brian looked down at her with a grin. He had positioned himself squarely in front of his uncle.

She took her chance. Running like a rabbit, she dashed for the door. Behind her, she heard a crash and some violent swearing, but by then she was out and pelting down the street as if the Giant Rat of Sumatra were after her. She leaped over the garbage in the alleyway and burst out onto the Main Street sidewalk, panting.

What time was it? How long had she been in the rat shop? The sky had turned cloudy, and it looked as if a storm were brewing. Ballet must be over by now, but maybe there was still time to sneak into French class and then walk out to meet Miss Barmy on the sidewalk.

On the sidewalk. There, half a block away, was a woman in a bulky raincoat, silhouetted against the gray sky. She was at the entrance to Emmy's French class, and she was tapping her foot.

Emmy longed to hide. If only she were a rat, she could crawl into that little crumbling hole on the side of those steps, by the concrete planter. It looked a perfect size . . .

"I don't think she went this way, Uncle!" Brian's voice echoed in the alley behind her.

Emmy flew across the road, ducked behind a bush, and peered through the leaves, shivering a little as a sudden cold gust swirled about her.

Brian's uncle poked his pinched face out of the alley, snarled in frustration, and turned back.

Good. Now all Emmy had to do was come up with an excuse for not being in French class. With any luck, Miss Barmy would only make her shampoo with oil of yak, or write a paper on better bowel habits through dietary empowerment, or read an article on the many exciting uses for tree balm.

There was a rustle of feet behind her. Emmy whipped around to face a pair of grass-stained soccer shorts.

"Hey!" Joe Benson squatted on his heels. "Listen, about that Rat—"

Emmy glanced over her shoulder. The woman in the coat was looking at her watch.

"What's going on?" Joe looked embarrassed, but determined. "Don't pretend you didn't hear the Rat talk, because I know you did."

"I'm not pretending," said Emmy hurriedly. "He does. He talks. I don't know why, either, but nobody else ever seems to hear him—"

"I did," said Joe.

"Yeah, well, you heard him today, but I've been hearing him all year." Emmy glanced nervously at the sky. It was going to rain any minute now. If she got wet, Miss Barmy would make her wrap up in about fifty blankets and sweat for an hour, to ward off a cold.

"All year? You haven't been in our class all year."

Emmy stared at him. "I've been sitting across from you since September," she said slowly.

"No way."

Emmy nodded. "I have. I was there on the first day of class. Don't you remember? The Rat bit me, and I yelled."

Joe shook his head.

"I was there when Mr. Herbifore tripped over the pumpkin in October, and when Robbie brought a snake to school the last day before Christmas break and it got lost, and in February when Kendra only got two valentines and she cried. And I saw you break your shoelace just last week and run around all day in your socks, and—"

"Okay, okay!" Joe ran a hand through his already messy hair. "But how come I can't remember *you?*"

"Emmaline Augusta, I see you behind that bush!"

Emmy whirled around. Steaming across the road was a broad, brisk woman with a mole on the end of her chin. Emmy almost melted with relief. It wasn't Miss Barmy after all.

"Emmaline *Augusta?*" Joe said in an undertone.

Emmy stood up. "I was named after two great-aunts," she muttered. "Don't rub it in."

"Why, *hello*, Mrs. Brecksniff!" Emmy put on her most winning smile.

"Don't you Mrs. Brecksniff me! Here it's Miss Barmy's afternoon off and I don't even know the proper time to come and get you, and now I see you dillydallying across the street without so much as a by-your-leave."

Joe coughed to hide what might have been a snicker. "Dillydallying?" he murmured as Mrs. Brecksniff neared.

Emmy ignored him. "I'm so sorry, Mrs. Brecksniff—"

"It's my fault, ma'am." Joe stepped forward. "Emmy and I are friends—"

Emmy looked at him in surprise.

"—and I had a question about a school project we're working on," Joe went on, shaking the housekeeper's plump hand in a businesslike manner.

"Joe!" A tall man beckoned from his car. "You need some more practice before supper!"

Joe grabbed his hair with both hands, looking exasperated. "We've got to figure this out," he said. "How about tomorrow? After school?"

"Emmaline is usually busy after school," said Mrs. Brecksniff. "What is your project about?"

Emmy looked blankly at Joe.

"Rats," said Joe promptly. "See you tomorrow, Emmy."

Emmy followed the housekeeper, who had a stride like a triathlete. If only she *could* meet Joe after school tomorrow . . . but of course she was busy. More than once, she had enviously watched the children who poured out of the school building at three o'clock into the free air, with nothing to do but play.

"Mrs. Brecksniff?" Emmy trotted alongside, slightly breathless. "Do you suppose my parents would mind if I didn't do so much after school?"

Mrs. Brecksniff turned, startled. "Your parents paid good money for those classes. Money isn't a thing to be wasted, even if you *are* rich."

"Yes, but—" Emmy tried again. "After a whole day of school, it gets so tiring. Do you think I could just quit ballet and French?"

"Certainly not."

"Well then, how about gymnastics? That's on Thursday."

"Out of the question."

"Pottery and tap dancing? Little theater? Tennis? Basket weaving?"

"Now see here, young lady." Mrs. Brecksniff looked down over her double chins. "Miss Barmy signed you up for all those things, and you know as well as I do what that means."

Emmy sighed. She knew.

"I don't care if she *is* my cousin, she's a nasty customer when crossed. It's a hard enough job that I have to do, what with nine bathrooms to clean, not to mention all those windows, and your parents flying in unexpectedly and having all those parties—"

Emmy looked up. Miss Barmy and Mrs. Brecksniff were cousins?

"—so don't complain to me. And I wouldn't complain to Miss Barmy either, or she might just sign you up for something else in the evening, too."

"I have to have some time to do homework," Emmy said sadly.

"And would that matter to her? It would not," said Mrs. Brecksniff, puffing out her neck until she looked like a stuffed frog. "Now hurry up, it's starting to rain. We'll be a couple of drowned rats before we get out of this."

The housekeeper churned determinedly down the hill, unfurling a large black umbrella as a peal of thunder crashed. She centered the umbrella directly over her rather ponderous bulk, so that Emmy had to stay very close indeed to be even partly protected.

And as the rain poured off the umbrella in a drip line that soaked her left shoulder, Emmy was not too cold and miserable and wet to spare a kind thought for the Rat, who *would* be nearly drowned out in this rain, and hope that he had finally found a squirrel who would let him in.

It was dark in Emmy's bedroom, but the storm had blown itself out at last, and as she watched from her window in the topmost turret, a final ragged cloud scudded across the bright face of the moon and vanished.

There was a brisk knock at Emmy's bedroom door. "Mrs. Brecksniff says to have a hot bath before bed," said a young woman, bringing in fresh towels. "I'll run it for you, honey."

"Thanks, Maggie," said Emmy, thinking how much she liked the new housemaid, who always had a smile. "But I can do it myself."

Maggie bent over the large Jacuzzi set in blue Italian tiles and turned on the faucets. "Honey, if I didn't do for people, I'd be out of a job." She smiled her wide, friendly smile, crooked teeth and big nose and all, and Emmy smiled right back.

"Now, I'll just lay out your pajamas, and— My stars!" Maggie, who had been rummaging in Emmy's pajama drawer, stopped with her head half turned. She was looking into the playroom.

Emmy felt her cheeks get hot. She hadn't asked for the toys, but they just kept coming. Her parents sent them from London and New York and every other place they went where she wasn't. There was a dollhouse with beds and wallpaper and chests full of doll clothes. There was an expensive model train set with a track that went through tunnels and mountains and all around the room, and a play kitchen, and an art center with a little sink for washing up, and an electronic keyboard, and a puppet theater, and every Lego set and stuffed animal imaginable.

Emmy looked at Maggie, embarrassed. "Can I go to bed now?"

Maggie turned swiftly. "Of course, sugar. Just pop yourself in the tub, and then tuck yourself in. Don't

forget to say your prayers, and I'll see you at breakfast. Do you like sausages?"

Emmy looked at her doubtfully. "The tofu kind?"
She had had experience with those.

"Over my dead body," Maggie said cheerfully.

Emmy threw on her pajamas and bounced into bed,
turning the picture on her bedside table so it caught
the moonlight. Her parents looked back at her.

Jim Addison was big and broad shouldered, with
eyes that crinkled at the corners. His arm was thrown
over his wife's shoulders, and Kathy Addison's soft
brown hair blew back against his sweater. She was
smiling right into the camera, her eyes warm.

They would look like that coming off the
plane. Her father would grin and ruffle her hair,
and her mother would swoop down and hug her
close. Then when they got home, her parents might
play a board game with her, or sit by the fire and
tell stories, or want to look at her school papers.
And they would say they were proud of her, and
that she was a good girl, and that they loved her
very much.

Emmy shut her eyes, happily snuggling deep under her blanket. But sleep wouldn't come.

What was so important about white fur behind a rat's ear? And did the rats in the store really have amazing powers? There had certainly been something very unusual about the Endear Mouse.

Emmy idly watched leaf shadows move and dance on the wall above her bed. How odd that there had been a rat in the store that looked so much like her own Rat. And then there was that awful rat man. She hadn't told him her last name, but might he find her anyway?

Emmy shuddered and quickly thought of something more pleasant. Joe. Now, there was a nice surprise. Someone who *noticed* her.

She gazed at the fluttering leaf shadows. It was good to have a friend. In fact, she had made three friends today, if you counted Brian and the Rat—

The leaves moved.

They had been moving all along, of course, but this movement was different. It was not the gentle fluttering of paper-thin shapes in a light breeze. It was the stealthy, purposeful movement of something alive. Something lumpy. Something that reached out one stubby finger and tapped.

Emmy stiffened.

The finger reached out again and tapped on the glass. Emmy looked closer. It wasn't a finger after all. It was a—

It was a stubby, short, furry foreleg with a paw attached—

It was the Rat.

5

"Rat!" Emmy ran to the window and creaked it open.

The Rat, wet and bedraggled, dragged himself over the sill and collapsed in a damp heap. His ear looked like it had been chewed.

"Where have you been?" Emmy whispered. "You look just—"

"Terrible," said the Rat, and sneezed. "I know."

"But what did you do? What happened to you?" Emmy carried him into her bathroom and set him gently on the counter. The Rat leaned against the blow-dryer and put his head in his paws.

"I have been chased. I have been beaten. I have been manhandled and taunted and set upon. Freedom," he added grimly, tossing back the lank and dripping fur that hung in his eyes, "has its bitter side."

"Oh, poor Rat!"

"And I'm cold and hungry, and I want a bath."

Emmy filled the sink and laid out a towel.

"Th—th—thang—" The Rat swallowed, hard, and cleared his throat.

"Thank you?" Emmy suggested.

The Rat nodded. The tip of his nose turned pink.

"You're welcome." Emmy tested the water in the sink. "So how did you ever find my house? And how did you know which window was mine?"

"You pointed it out, remember?" The Rat's tone was impatient. "Topmost turret, blue window. I just climbed up the grapevine."

"Oh," said Emmy.

There was a little silence. The Rat tapped his foot.

"Look," he burst out at last, irritably. "Is it the usual thing for you to watch your guests take a bath? Because if it isn't, then why don't you just go get me something to eat—*not* rat pellets—and give me a little privacy?"

Emmy was almost down the back stairs to the kitchen when she heard the voice she dreaded above all.

"So you didn't meet Emmaline coming out of French? Where was she, exactly?"

Emmy stopped, paralyzed. Should she try to get

back up the stairs without being heard? But some of the steps creaked. . . . Undecided, she looked down. The old-fashioned staircase turned a corner just before descending to the kitchen, and a wedge of light crossed the steps just below Emmy's feet. She could see Mrs. Brecksniff's bulky shadow, her hands on her substantial hips.

"She was right across the street," said Mrs. Brecksniff, sounding defensive. "There was no danger, she was just talking to a friend."

"A *friend?*" Miss Barmy's voice scaled up dangerously.

"Nothing wrong with friends, last I heard," said Mrs. Brecksniff stoutly. "The poor girl could use a few more of them."

There was a long, dangerous silence.

"Any friends must be approved by *me*," said Miss Barmy coldly. "Emmaline has been troublesome lately—influenced, no doubt, by this so-called friend. Or perhaps," she added, her voice silky, "Emmaline has been getting encouragement from *you*."

"Now, Jane Barmy, there's no call to take that tone with me." Mrs. Brecksniff made a noise that sounded like an irritated buffalo.

"The girl's health is delicate, and I will allow no interference." Miss Barmy's voice was crisp.

"I'm not—"

"Her medicines must be carefully calibrated to her exact emotional condition. I was forced to create an entirely new batch and bring it to her at school."

"Well I'm sure I don't know what you're so worried about," Mrs. Brecksniff burst out passionately. "You don't care about Emmy, you've made that plain—"

"That's enough, now, you're talking wild—"

"—all you care about is the Addison money, and I know that you'd just as soon she was out of the way altogether—"

"STOP!"

Emmy's knees were suddenly trembling.

"Not one word more, Rebecca Brecksniff. I can get you fired tomorrow!"

"I know you can, more's the pity," Mrs. Brecksniff went on hysterically. "The girl's parents listen to you— who knows why—you'd never dare talk like this in front of your mother, or your poor dear father—your mother knew what it was to be housekeeper of this house, what with managing the staff and keeping nine bathrooms clean, not to mention the windows—"

Mrs. Brecksniff was making a great deal of noise, honking and blowing into her handkerchief. Emmy gripped the stair treads with hands that felt strangely cold. She had never felt that Miss Barmy really liked her; but to actually want her out of the way? Could Mrs. Brecksniff be right?

"Stop sniveling," Miss Barmy said icily. "Control yourself now. The girl's parents are arriving tomorrow night, and . . ."

Miss Barmy's voice faded as the women moved off. Emmy strained to hear, but the only word she caught was "potato."

She waited until the voices had faded entirely. Then, cautiously, she poked her head around the corner. The coast was clear, and she still had to get the Rat something to eat.

What did rats like to eat?

On the counter was Miss Barmy's health food, neatly labeled. Emmy shuddered, pocketing an apple and a box of raisins instead. She risked a look in the fridge—weren't rats supposed to like cheese? But she didn't dare take time to cut a slice . . . there! Maggie kept a stash of candy behind the breadbox. Emmy snatched a peanut-butter cup and fled up the stairs.

On the second-floor landing she heard Miss Barmy's voice raised in the foyer below.

"No, I insist. You *must* keep the rest of the servants out of the kitchen while I'm baking. It's an old family recipe—and the ingredients are secret."

Emmy stood in the shadows, suddenly thoughtful. It was the same thing every time her parents came home: Miss Barmy had to bake her special potato rolls. But why?

Emmy stole quietly up the stairs to her bedroom. A whooshing sound was coming from the bathroom, and she cracked open the door.

The blow-dryer, lying on its side, had been turned on. A tube of hair gel was oozing green. And standing happily in front of the mirror, looking remarkably spiky, was the Rat.

"So what's for breakfast around here? Toast points with mushrooms? Eggs Benedict?"

Emmy opened her eyes and choked back a scream. The Rat was sitting on her chest, his sharp, whiskered face just inches from her nose.

She sat up, tumbling the Rat among the blankets. "Breakfast is usually cereal. Or, if Maggie cooks, maybe sausages. What are you talking about? In your cage, all you ate were those little pellets."

"A rodent can dream, can't he?" The Rat's ears turned pink.

"But where did you ever hear about toast points and all that? You've been locked in a cage for years."

"I took advantage of my educational opportunities," said the Rat stiffly. "In short, I learned to read. It would have been hard to avoid, after years in an elementary classroom. Not only that but I know the Pledge of Allegiance, and 'America the Beautiful,' and all the words to 'The Star-Spangled Banner.'"

"But toast points? Eggs Benedict?"

The Rat looked uncomfortable. "Well, if you must know," he said, "every time the paper in my cage was changed, I had something new to read. If the teacher did it, I mostly got *Teacher's Tattle*. But if I was home with a student for the weekend, I got a little bit of everything." The Rat lowered his voice. "Some kids got the *National Snooper*. Did you know that the English royal family are really descendants of Martians? And that Elvis has been reincarnated as a hound dog?"

Emmy grinned.

"I got stock tips from the *New York Drone,* and I was very interested in *Psychology Piffle.* But my favorite was *Nummi Gourmet.* Those pictures of chocolate mousse—*mmmm*—and toast points . . .

"Speaking of which—" The Rat's tone sharpened. "What was it you said about sausages?"

"I'll see what I can bring back from breakfast. But I've got to hurry. And you'd better keep out of sight."

The Rat sat on Emmy's dresser and licked the last bit of breakfast sausage off his paws. "Excellent flavor," he remarked. "But a little heavy on the lint. Did you have to put them in your pocket?"

"Yes," said Emmy briefly, stuffing her homework into her backpack. It hadn't been easy, sneaking them off her plate under the watchful eye of Mrs. Brecksniff—not to mention the cat, Muffy, who had a strong liking for sausages and a very persistent meow.

"Weren't there any peanut-butter cups?"

"For *breakfast?*"

"Why not?" The Rat skipped nimbly onto Emmy's arm and ran over her shoulder. Emmy felt a little thump and a rummaging sort of feeling inside the pack on her back. "Just drop me off outside, will you?"

Emmy shut the bedroom door behind her. "You think you'll have better luck with the squirrels in my yard?"

"I couldn't have worse," the Rat said grumpily. "That squirrel yesterday was an absolute moron. And the chipmunks weren't much better. I could barely understand them, and *they* certainly didn't understand *me*." A little worry crept into the Rat's voice. "Perhaps I haven't been educated properly. Maybe *Teacher's Tattle* was right—American schools *should* offer more languages."

Emmy started down the stairs as the Rat burst out again, fretfully. "How can I be a star, a high-achieving rat, when I've never even studied Rodentese?"

Emmy shrugged. "Nobody expects you to be anything more than an ordinary rat, as far as I know."

The Rat gave an incredulous snort. "And are *you* content to be just an ordinary girl?"

Emmy trailed her hand along the smooth wood of the banister, wishing she dared slide down it. If she were an ordinary girl, she would. If she were an ordinary girl, she'd have parents at home and cake on her birthday.

"I wouldn't mind being ordinary," Emmy said.

"And that," said the Rat darkly, "is yet another flaw in the American school system. Low expectations. Leading—yourself as a prime example—to drab, ordinary children. Oh, the shame . . ."

Emmy took the last four steps in one leap and landed in the kitchen with a bounce that shook the Rat into silence.

"Is this my lunch, Maggie? Are there any peanut-butter cups?"

"*Peanut-butter cups?*" Miss Barmy appeared in the doorway, abruptly reaching for the bag. "I've told you before, I won't have this child poisoning herself with sugar! Now, what happened to those tofu muffins?" She rummaged in the refrigerator as she spoke, pulling out bran bars. "*This* is the food a growing child needs."

Maggie glanced pityingly at Emmy as Miss Barmy repacked the lunch bag with a great noise of crinkling paper. The Rat poked his head out to see the commotion, uttered a distressed squeak, and fell back in again.

Emmy felt something brush against her leg. It was the cat.

"Oh, go away, you," Emmy muttered. Muffy, staring earnestly at the backpack, began to meow.

"There!" Miss Barmy held out the lunch sack. "Why, whatever is the matter with that cat? It seems to be staring at your—"

"Miss Barmy!" Emmy interrupted hurriedly. "Did you have a nice day out yesterday? Where did you go?" She opened her eyes wide.

A little muscle jumped at the corner of Miss Barmy's eye. "Nowhere in particular," she said vaguely. "Dear me, we mustn't forget our herbal scent on the pulse points." She took a small bottle from her sleeve, shaking it fussily.

Emmy smiled with secret joy. She had just discovered something: the way to keep the nanny from being too nosy about Emmy's business was to ask questions about things Miss Barmy would rather keep hidden!

The nanny dabbed a little liquid behind Emmy's

ears. "The lovely scent will linger all day, providing a pleasant respite from the rigors of study."

Emmy, by a wrenching effort, managed to avoid rolling her eyes. Of all Miss Barmy's weird herbal remedies, this was the most pointless. The scent that she dabbed on didn't even smell particularly nice—and after the first few minutes, Emmy didn't notice it at all.

Miss Barmy sipped her prune juice, humming a little under her breath. "Don't forget, Emmaline—tonight is quality time with your parents. It's on the schedule—fifteen minutes, or perhaps more if you're good."

"Yes, ma'am," said Emmy, turning to go. Fifteen minutes' quality time—she'd get a lot more than that. Just the ride from the airport was thirty minutes, at least!

Maggie held the back door open and winked. And as Emmy passed outside, she felt something being dropped quietly into her pocket.

Two peanut-butter cups.

6

EMMY OPENED HER BACKPACK behind the hedge. "Climb out—I'm going to be late for school."

"Is it safe?" The Rat peered up, squinting in the sudden light. "I nearly had a heart attack when I saw that—"

"*Meow?*" A furry golden head pushed past Emmy's arm to peer into the backpack. The Rat tumbled over in a dead faint.

"Oh, great, Muffy." Emmy pushed the cat away with an impatient hand. "Scare him to death, why don't you?"

The cat looked smug.

"Well, I'll have to take him to school now," said Emmy. "No thanks to you." She hoisted the pack and took off at a run. She slid into her seat just as the last bell rang, undid the top flap of her backpack, and risked a whisper.

"Rat!"

No answer.

Worried, Emmy got a bathroom pass and took her backpack with her. "Ratty? Speak to me!"

The Rat moaned from the depths of the pack. "Did you have to run the whole way?"

"Oh, Rat, I'm sorry—"

He put a paw to his head. "I felt like cement in a mixer. And my heart is still racing from that . . . that . . . *what* did you call that cat?"

"Muffy," Emmy said miserably.

"Muffy?" the Rat repeated in tones of disbelief. "Not *Fang*? Not *Assassin*?" He shook his head and looked around. "What is this place?"

"The girls' bathroom," Emmy said. "At school."

"*School?*" the Rat shrieked. "You take me back to my *prison?*"

"Listen. You can take a nap"—Emmy looked around for inspiration—"in a soft nest," she finished, crumpling some toilet paper in the bottom of her backpack. "I'll drop in something to eat at lunchtime. Come on, get in."

The Rat looked sourly at her. "I'm hungry now. Is your lunch in that sack?"

"You can have it. Have anything you want. Just *hurry.*"

The Rat poked his nose into the lunch bag. "Hmm, this looks interesting." He took a bite, chewed, and stopped, looking distressed. "Great rat droppings, what *is* this slop?"

"Tofu muffin. Sorry. It wasn't my idea."

"No peanut-butter cups?"

Emmy put her hand in her pocket and hesitated. "First promise me that you'll stay in my backpack all day."

"Scout's honor," the Rat said, holding up a paw.

Emmy looked at him. "You're not a Scout."

"As good as," the Rat said. "They held Scout meetings in that classroom every week after school for as long as I can remember. I can tie all the knots—"

"All right," said Emmy, cutting him short. "Get in."

"Where's my peanut-butter cup?"

Emmy handed one in. "Don't make any noise," she warned, but the Rat was too busy chewing to answer.

Emmy pushed back hot bangs from her sweaty forehead. A smell of cut grass drifted in as a lawn mower droned outside, and Mr. Herbifore looked warm and bored as he lectured on the exports of Asia. The class listened with glazed eyes, half asleep.

Emmy, however, was wide awake. She had to be, to cover up the noise the Rat was making.

There he went, rustling again! Emmy faked a cough, wondering for the seventeenth time why the Rat couldn't just lie still. Weren't rodents supposed to be nocturnal? Why couldn't this one sleep all day?

Emmy tried not to look at the Rat's empty cage. No one had seemed to notice that he was missing, but it was only a matter of time, and the knowledge gave her a horrible sense of impending doom.

A noise of slamming books and banging desktops gave Emmy the cover she needed. She bent over her backpack as if to take out the assignment that Mr. Herbifore had just called for.

"Will you *please* be quiet?" she hissed.

The Rat turned a despairing face upward. "But I'm so hot," he quavered. "I'm *baking* in here, and no one *cares*."

"We're all hot," said Emmy impatiently, "but you're the only one I hear moaning. And what was that ripping sound?"

The Rat waved a pleated bit of white paper. "I only made a fan."

Emmy felt exasperated. "Out of my homework?"

Two large brown shoes came into view and stopped beside Emmy's desk. "Your poetry assignment?"

"Um . . ." Emmy didn't look up at Mr. Herbifore as she pulled a sheet of lined paper from her backpack. At the top, neatly written, was her name. A jagged edge was all that was left of the lower right corner.

Mr. Herbifore looked critically at the paper as a shadow passed by the window. Emmy glanced out, half seeing a small, stooped figure duck behind the lilac bushes. Had the school hired a new gardener?

"This is hardly acceptable," said the teacher. "What's your excuse? The cat chewed it?"

Emmy felt like strangling the Rat.

"Stay after school and copy it over. Five points off for messiness."

"Thanks a lot," Emmy whispered bitterly into her backpack when it was safe.

"Would you rather I died of heatstroke?" The Rat sniffed. "At least in my cage I had a water dish and the breeze from the window."

"Fine," said Emmy. "I'll put you back in. You've been nothing but trouble ever since I set you free."

Ignoring the Rat's sudden look of dismay, she set the pack on the floor but relented enough to open the top flap a crack. She glanced up—and caught Joe staring at the backpack with unusual interest.

"... And so poetry is an expression of one's deeper emotions," the teacher intoned, still shuffling through the papers he had collected. "I'll read a few aloud, and let's see if we can discover what the author was really saying. Here's an interesting one. 'I always have to practice hard, even out in my back yard—' "

Out in the hall, there was a sound of footsteps, and a shadowy figure paused in the doorway. Emmy looked up.

A small man stepped forward, passed a bony hand over thinning brown hair, and peered into the classroom.

Emmy's heart gave a bump.

It was Professor Vole.

"Yes? May I help you with something?" asked Mr. Herbifore.

Emmy slid down in her seat. How had he known where to find her? And what would he do when he saw the Rat's cage was empty? Emmy felt a sudden stillness in her middle—and the Rat chose that moment to squeak.

Luckily, Joe dropped a book immediately afterward.

Emmy opened the lid of her desk and lifted her backpack as if to rummage in it. Hidden behind the open desk top, she frowned fiercely.

"*Will—you—be—quiet?*"

"But . . . but . . ." The Rat was shaking. "I heard a voice. It scares me! I remember—"

Emmy watched as the Rat twisted his paws together anxiously. "What do you remember?" She glanced quickly at the doorway, where Mr. Herbifore and Brian's uncle were still talking.

"I was just a little ratling in the nest—me and Sissy together. Our mother was gone—just for a minute, she said—and then I heard that voice! And then the big hand came and scooped us up! I bit it, too—I did—but then it squished me—the big, bony hand! *The big hand!*"

Emmy gave the Rat a little shake. "*Hush!*" she whispered fiercely, slipping the pack to the floor just as Mr. Herbifore turned.

"You're welcome to look at our rat," he was saying, "but I've had him for years. I found him shivering in the schoolyard and kept him for a class pet."

"It was years ago that I lost him," the professor said in his reedy voice, following Mr. Herbifore like a black, musty shadow.

The professor, his thin face eager, never glanced Emmy's way. He walked down the window aisle and stopped, his eyes devouring the cage.

"That's odd," said Mr. Herbifore. "He's usually active at this time of day. Perhaps he's hiding. I'll check inside his shelter."

"Stop!" The rat man's voice was anxious. "You mustn't let yourself be bitten! Just give me the cage."

"My dear sir!" Mr. Herbifore sounded affronted. "I can handle a mere rodent. After all, I'm a *teacher*—"

"And I am a professor, my dear sir, and I'm telling you, you must not be bitten! I will *not* answer for the consequences!"

Emmy's heart had begun a slow, hard pounding. She risked a glance at her backpack and stiffened. The Rat was peeking out. His nose twitched as he sniffed the air—and then he caught sight of Professor Vole.

There was a soft thud as the Rat fell back into the depths of the pack.

Emmy heard a sound like a snarling dog. Only it wasn't a dog at all. It was the rat man, and he was looking straight at her.

7

"YOU LITTLE THIEF," Professor Vole rasped, low in his throat. "Where's my rat?"

"Now, just a minute!" The indignant voice of Mr. Herbifore came over the roaring in Emmy's ears.

Professor Vole twisted around. "She was in my shop yesterday, telling me about this rat," he said, in his thin, reedy voice, now taut with anger. "And now he's gone!"

Mr. Herbifore straightened, frowning. "Why is this one rat so important? Surely you can buy another at any pet store—and you might get one that's better tempered."

"Another rat?" The rat man stared. "That rat was *irreplaceable*. You have absolutely no *conception* of its value." He fixed Emmy with his pale eyes. *"What have you done with my rat?"*

Emmy lifted her chin and glared right back. A new and unaccustomed spirit of defiance was stinging in her veins. So she had set the Rat free. So what?

The Rat was his own creature—not just a piece of property!

"HEY!" Professor Vole grabbed her desktop and wrenched it open. "Trying to *hide* him, are you?"

Emmy's heart gave a sudden, violent leap. She shrank back against her chair as the man's big, bony hands made a jumble of the papers inside her desk, spilling them onto the floor. She felt, rather than saw, Joe move from his seat to pick up the scattered papers in the aisle.

"Stop this instant!" Mr. Herbifore's voice scaled up. "Leave that girl alone; she wouldn't do anything against the rules, you hardly even know she's there most days—"

The rat man showed his small, white teeth in an alarming grin. "Ah *ha!* You've got him in your *backpack!*"

He made a sudden pounce, pulled the backpack from under Emmy's desk, and tossed out the contents in one violent motion. Papers fluttered as Mr. Herbifore squawked in outrage. Emmy, frozen, could only stare.

But there was no shout of triumph from Professor Vole, no frightened squeak from the Rat. There was just a blank silence as the rat man stood, staring at the empty pack as if he had been cheated.

"There! Are you satisfied now? Get out of my room this instant!" The teacher grasped the little man firmly by the arm and propelled him toward the door.

Emmy looked down at the mess, dazed. And then her eyes focused on unfamiliar handwriting. These weren't her papers! The name at the top of the pages was "Joe Benson." It had been *Joe's* backpack the old man had ransacked!

But then where was hers? Emmy looked across the aisle at Joe, who grinned triumphantly, clasping his hands over his head like a victorious boxer.

"I saw that!" The rat man, purple with rage, struggled in Mr. Herbifore's grip. "That boy—*he* stole my rat! Look in *his* backpack! Give back my rat, or I'll sue the whole school!"

Mr. Herbifore looked suddenly nervous. "You'll have to discuss that with the principal. But," he added, his voice growing a little stronger, "I will *not* tolerate threats or further searches of student property. That behavior is . . . Inappropriate. It's . . . Unacceptable! It's . . . just . . . plain . . ."

Mr. Herbifore stopped, his face red. He seemed to be wrestling with himself. "*I'm* tolerant," he muttered, "*I* never make negative value judgments or verbalize blame." His voice rose, and he threw back his head. "I haven't used a single banned word since being requalified by the Institute of Nice Educators and Pleasant Teachers. But I don't *care* anymore. I'm going to *say* it. Your behavior is just—plain—"

"Well?" said Professor Vole.

"It's BAD!" Mr. Herbifore burst out passionately. "It's WRONG! And you should be ASHAMED OF YOURSELF!"

Professor Vole looked suddenly smaller.

"Oh, the RELIEF!" cried the teacher, jabbing the professor's chest with his finger. "To finally be able to SAY it!"

The professor backed up with each jab, stumbling over his feet. The children watched in fascination as, with one last emphatic shove, Mr. Herbifore pushed the man out the door, slammed it hard, and picked up the phone.

"Take out your workbooks and do page 47," he said over his shoulder. "Oh, yes. I'd like to speak to the principal immediately," he said into the phone.

Emmy, stunned—she hadn't known Mr. Herbifore had it in him—sneaked a look at Joe as she reached for her workbook. A warm, grateful feeling bloomed as she saw her backpack safe under his desk. Good old Joe.

She flashed a victory sign and Joe grinned, glancing at the pack. And then his face took on a look of dismay. Seeping out from the bottom of Emmy's pack, and wetting the bottom of Joe's shoes, was a spreading yellow puddle.

The Rat, in his terror, had peed.

Meg, the girl who sat in front of Emmy, helped her pick up the scattered papers. "Weren't you scared?" she whispered.

"To death," Emmy whispered back. It was such a natural exchange that she didn't realize what had just happened until the girl turned back to her desk.

Another kid besides Joe had actually spoken to her!

So maybe Professor Vole's visit hadn't been all bad. At least the other kids could hardly pretend she didn't exist, now that she'd been screamed at by a demented maniac and accused of rodent stealing.

Across the aisle, Joe ripped a page from his notebook and dropped it to the floor, looking hunted. Emmy watched as the crisp white paper turned limp and yellow, blotting up the puddle at the base of her backpack. Joe was going to need more paper; it was amazing how much pee one small Rat could hold. But there was something else amazing about the Rat, and Professor Vole knew what it was. If the Rat were in the back room at the Antique Rat, what would his tag say? "The Talking Rat"?

Emmy grinned a little. That might not be so very valuable. After all, what the Rat said was usually obnoxious.

Still, Brian's uncle could probably sell a talking rat for a lot of money. Even the Endear Mouse, though clearly intelligent, hadn't seemed able to speak.

Or was it something else that made the Rat so special? Something more?

Emmy stared hard at math problem number 59. "A car is traveling at sixty feet per second . . ."

What would Professor Vole put on the Rat's tag?

The other rat, with the white patch behind its right ear, had something written on its tag . . . "The

Shrinking Rat," that was it. But what did that mean? That the rat got smaller? *That* wouldn't be much use to anyone.

The bell rang. The classroom was suddenly noisy with banging desktops and voices.

"Hurry up, Joe!"

"C'mon, big game today!"

Emmy shoved Joe's backpack under his desk and grabbed her own in the commotion.

"Hey, maybe he's got the rat, like that crazy old man said."

"Yeah, Joe—tell us what you did with the rat!"

Emmy shrugged. She could talk to Joe another time.

"Bye, Emmy—see you tomorrow!"

Meg gave a shy wave as she passed Emmy on her way out the door. Emmy managed to wave back in spite of her amazement at being spoken to yet again.

"Emmy?" Mr. Herbifore's voice stopped her. "Did you remember that you were supposed to stay after school and copy your poem over?"

Emmy stared at her teacher. What was this, a new trend? He'd remembered her name twice in a row.

Mr. Herbifore's face softened. "I don't mean to be hard on you, Emmy. Your work has been good in the past. But that's no reason to be slack now, is it?"

Emmy shook her head.

"Good. Oh, and one more thing." Mr. Herbifore leaned over his desk and looked at her kindly. "I don't for one minute think you took that man's rat— if it *was* his."

Emmy remained guiltily silent.

"In fact"—Mr. Herbifore paused, his face rather red—"I should have stopped him sooner. And now that I think about it, let's forget about you doing your assignment over. Accidents happen. Just hand it in to me as it is."

Emmy thought quickly. She had put the poetry assignment in her backpack. It was probably drenched in rat pee.

"No, thank you, Mr. Herbifore," she said. "I'd rather copy it over. Really."

Emmy worked carefully at her desk. She tried not to look out the window where Joe's team was warming up, or at the playground where lucky children, free for the day, played on the swings and monkey bars.

"I have to leave for a moment," Mr. Herbifore said. "Just put the assignment on my desk when you're done."

Emmy nodded. She was finishing up when the Rat poked his nose cautiously out of the pack.

"Is he gone?" the Rat whispered hoarsely. "Is the bad man gone?"

"All gone," said Emmy. "Get back in the pack, will you? I've got to go to gymnastics."

The Rat hesitated, looking behind his tail into the depths of the pack. The skin under his fur flushed pink. "I . . . I'd rather not, if you don't mind. It's a little damp in there." He twisted the end of his tail nervously between his paws, lifted his chin, and gazed at a point just beyond Emmy's left shoulder.

"Damp?" said Emmy, keeping a straight face with an effort. She was enjoying this.

"I believe," said the Rat, his ears turning crimson, "that it's not unusual for rodents to sweat a great deal—especially when they're anxious." He shot such a worried glance at Emmy that she didn't have the heart to embarrass him further.

"Of course," she said quickly. "Ride in the side pocket, then. We have to hurry or I'm going to be late to gymnastics."

The Rat climbed into the pocket with remarkable haste and hid his head in his paws. He didn't quite fit, and Emmy tucked his tail in tenderly. Poor Rat. He'd had a terrible day.

Holding the backpack at arm's length, she dropped her paper on the teacher's desk. She caught sight of Joe's poem, right on top.

His printing was bold and very clear. Surely it was all right to look at the one that the teacher had already read aloud? It was titled "To Dad."

> I always have to practice hard
> Even out in my back yard.
> You make me do it every day.
> Can't you let me—just play?

Emmy blinked. So she wasn't the only one with parent trouble?

And then she saw the envelope next to Joe's paper.

It was pink, with the address written in an elegant script that she had seen many times before.

Emmy snatched it from the desk and opened the letter. It might be snooping, but finding out what Miss Barmy had written to her teacher was a matter of survival. She scanned it quickly.

Dear Mr. Herbifore,

I certainly understand why you had to cancel; nevertheless, I am sure the children are terribly disappointed—they always love my visits, and of course the atmostherapy I provide is so soothing. So I shall arrive on Friday, at one o'clock sharp, with another very special experience for the class to enjoy during silent-reading time, compliments of the Addison family.

Yours sincerely,

Jane A. Barmy

"Pssst! Hurry up!" The Rat's paw emerged from the pocket and tapped her wrist with his pointed claws.

Emmy didn't even flinch. She stared at the paper in her hand as footsteps sounded in the hall.

"Teacher's coming," the Rat sang out. Emmy crammed the letter back in the envelope with shaking hands. What did it all mean? Not once, as far as Emmy knew, had Miss Barmy *ever* come into the classroom during silent-reading time. And what on earth was *atmostherapy*? There was something very peculiar about Miss Barmy. . . .

8

EMMY ALMOST CRASHED into Dr. Leander in her hurry to get out of the building.

"Oh, hello," he said. "Feeling better, are we?"

"Um," said Emmy, ducking behind him. She had just seen the rat man coming down the hall, led by the principal.

The Rat had seen him, too. There was a frightened squeak from the backpack's pocket, and a sudden scrabbling of claws up Emmy's arm. She nearly yelped aloud.

"*Get—your claws—off—my neck!*" Emmy hissed, trying to disengage the Rat, who had hidden under her hair.

"What did you say, Emmaline?" The psychologist took out a blue notebook and flipped a page.

Emmy backed out the door, wedging her fingers beneath the Rat's tightly gripping paws. "Nothing, Dr. Leander—*ouch!*"

Dr. Leander followed her outside, writing busily. "Do you talk to yourself often, dear?"

Emmy gave the Rat's body a little furious shake. "Oh—you know—now and then. When I'm really *annoyed*, or in *pain*—"

"Are you troubled about something, perhaps? Do you think someone is out to get you?"

"Someone just *got* me," said Emmy through her teeth as she pulled the Rat off her neck with a wrench that felt like it drew blood. "And someone else"—she gave Dr. Leander a hunted look—"keeps *following* me."

She thrust the Rat into her backpack, but he wouldn't let go.

"Who keeps following you, Emmaline?" Dr. Leander kept his head down, writing as he trotted alongside. "Tell me."

Emmy gave him an exasperated glare. "A giant brain-sucking spider. A ten-foot-tall noodle. Write anything you want, but I'*m* going to gymnastics!"

"Talks to self . . . hallucinations," muttered the psychologist, taking notes as Emmy stalked off. "Becomes hostile when questioned. . . ."

Emmy was halfway across the playground before she managed to free her hand from the Rat's death grip. "Did you have to get hysterical?"

"I was not hysterical." The Rat had regained his dignified bearing. "I was merely reacting with the natural instinct of the hunted animal. Instinct, I might add, is something very understandable in a—"

"Chicken?" Emmy felt the back of her neck tenderly.

"—in a creature that must live by his wits and—"

"Feathers?"

"Oh, shut up," said the Rat grumpily. "Anyway, *you're* the one who's so *troubled*. Why do you go to see that guy, anyway? Been torturing frogs? Hearing voices?"

"Miss Barmy makes me. You know, my nanny."

"Whatever for?"

Emmy glanced over at the soccer game. "Oh, she says my mental health is important, and it's just like a regular checkup at the doctor's, or something."

"And you believe that?" The Rat sounded disdainful.

"Not really, but I don't care if I skip class—it's only during silent reading, anyway."

"Hey, Joe! Nice footwork!"

Emmy walked behind the crowd on the sidelines. They were cheering, but Joe's father was the loudest of all. He strode up and down, waving his arms.

"That's my boy! Come on, go, go, GO!"

Joe's father was laughing, his face full of satisfaction, and Emmy felt a moment of pure envy. Maybe Joe's dad did make him practice hard, like it said in the poem, but he sure was proud of his son.

Oh, well. Her parents would be home tonight, and maybe they would be proud of her, too. She had saved all her tests, and her essay titled "Animals of India," and her latest report card. She imagined their faces when they saw all the A's. Should she show her schoolwork in the car? Or during quality time at home? No—maybe she'd just tie the whole packet up with a ribbon and hand it to her parents at bedtime . . .

"NO! Follow the player, not the ball—listen, you STUPID KID!"

Joe's father paced. His neck was swollen, and the pride on his face had changed to dark red anger.

Emmy didn't want to look at Joe. Now she understood the poem he had written.

But she had problems of her own. Through the shoulders of the crowd, she could see a man in black coming out of the school, looking around.

Emmy's eyes slid sideways to the belt of trees and bushes that edged the school property. She waited until the man turned away, shading his eyes. And then, like a rabbit, she bolted for the safety of the trees.

"Why did you run? Did you see the bad man again?" The Rat's tremulous voice wafted up from her backpack as soon as she set it down.

"Yes," said Emmy, crouched low behind the bushes, "but I found a place to hide."

"It's not dark enough," said the Rat worriedly. "Can't you find a nice hole somewhere?"

Emmy peered anxiously through the leaves. Where was Professor Vole now? She turned back to see the Rat's small, plump body clamber out of the pocket. "Ratty, don't run off!"

"Call of nature," said the Rat briefly, moving to a nearby tree and lifting his hind leg. "Do you *mind*?"

He glared until Emmy looked away—and then, all at once, a whistle blew, a player shouted, and a black-

and-white ball came crashing through the bushes. It landed just behind Emmy, spinning.

"I'll get it!" a familiar voice called, and in the next instant two sturdy legs pounded into the brush. In the space of a breath, Joe tripped over Emmy, tumbled in a wild thrashing of bare arms and blue jersey and one flying shoe, and landed a solid elbow right on the Rat's long, pink tail.

The Rat screamed and snapped in automatic reflex, biting Joe in the biceps. A drop of blood welled up and Joe stared at his arm, his face very pale.

"I . . . don't feel so good," he whispered. "I feel . . . really weird."

"I feel worse," gasped the Rat, still holding his damaged tail. And then he didn't say any more, for Joe began to shrink.

Right before their eyes, without any warning at all, Joe shrank to the size of the Rat. His clothes shrank with him, all except for the shoe that had fallen off in his wild tumble. Joe stared at it—a black soccer shoe, bigger than his whole body—with the expression of a shock victim.

"Joe! Where are you? Did you get the ball?"

Feet thudded. Voices called. The Rat stood with his paws in his mouth, staring at Joe.

There was no time to think, so Emmy acted on instinct alone. She stuffed Joe and the Rat into her backpack, curled up on the ground, and shut her eyes.

9

Amid the sudden babble of voices, Emmy lay still.

"Are you all right, little girl? What happened?"

"Did you see a boy come through here?"

Emmy put a hand weakly to her head and tried for a dazed expression. It wasn't hard. "Yes, but . . ." She trailed off, looking around her. "I don't see him."

"Here's his shoe," said one of the men, looking grim. Joe's father ran into the road, looking up and down Main Street. "Joe! Joe!"

"A kid can't just disappear," said someone.

"Not without help," said another voice. "Did anyone see a car stop?"

There was a silence.

"All right," said the referee. "Somebody call the police. The rest of you fan out and search."

Emmy pulled the backpack from under the bushes and stood up.

"Joe!" she called, along with fifty others. "Joe!" She walked across the street and into the entrance to the gym. Through the glass she could see her class practicing on the uneven parallel bars, but Emmy went straight up the stairs to the girls' bathroom, entered a stall, and locked the door.

The Rat stuck his head out, looking disgusted. "Don't tell me—we're in another girls' bathroom. Sheesh!"

Emmy opened the top flap and looked in nervously. "Joe? Are you okay?"

"Okay? *Okay?* I'm shorter than a Barbie doll, I'm stuffed inside a backpack with a rat, and you ask me if I'm *okay?* You're joking, right?"

Joe pulled down the side zipper and stuck his head out, breathing deeply. "That's better. No offense, but your backpack really reeks. What is that awful smell?"

Emmy looked at the Rat, who crimsoned deeply under his fur.

"Oh no." Joe looked from one to the other. "Oh no no no—I remember now—"

Emmy and the Rat both spoke at once.

"I tried to mop it up—"

"It was just a little sweat—"

Joe shuddered, looking like Tom Thumb in a soccer jersey, and shut his eyes. "This has *got* to be a dream."

"Don't be so sure," said Emmy gloomily. She looked at Joe—a tiny person with a disgusted expression—and found that the impossible was not so hard to believe anymore. Maybe she was getting used to it. She had believed in a talking Rat for long enough, after all. What was so amazing about a shrinking boy? Or no—it was a shrinking *rat*, the tag had said.

"But it's too bizarre to be real!" Joe looked darkly at the Rat. "What did you bite me for, anyway? Were you *trying* to shrink me?"

The Rat looked sulky. "You'd bite somebody, too, if they creamed your tail." He lifted his tail and examined it tenderly. "Anyway, how come you think it was *my* fault?"

"But it was!" Emmy sounded excited.

"Oh, sure," said the Rat hotly, "blame the rodent, as usual."

"No, listen. That tag—on the other rat in the store, the one just like you—I didn't understand it at first, but now it all makes sense. You're a Shrinking Rat."

"A *what*?"

"A Shrinking Rat. Of Schenectady, whatever that means." Emmy grinned. "That's why the rat man wanted you back. You bite people, they shrink. You're just like that other rat in the store—"

"But that can't be right." Joe frowned in concentration. "He bit me yesterday when I tried to feed him, and nothing happened then."

"What rat in what store?" The Rat looked from Emmy to Joe and back again.

"Anyway," said Joe, looking indignant, "if Ratso here *did* shrink me, then he can just unshrink me right now. No way am I going to spend the rest of my life the size of a Batman action figure."

"*Unshrink* you?" the Rat screeched. "What do you think I am, a *magician*?"

"Guys!" Emmy nudged them back inside the pack. "We can't sit here arguing in the bathroom forever. We've got to *think*. Who can help us? What are we going to do?"

"It still stinks in here," Joe said irritably, but Emmy ignored him. Cautiously, she peeked around the corner.

There was no one on the landing. But through the second-floor window, Emmy could see flashing lights. There were police cars. There was Joe's father, holding his son's shoe. And there was someone in black, surrounded by officers in uniform.

Emmy slid open the window a crack and listened.

"That's him!" cried Mr. Herbifore. "That's the man who threatened Joe, right in my classroom! If anyone took the boy, he did!"

"I need that rat for research!" shouted Professor Vole. "You're interfering with the pursuits of science! I demand my rights!"

"Here are your rights," said a burly policeman. "You have the right to remain silent. Anything you say can and will be used against you. . . ."

Emmy watched as Professor Vole was handcuffed, put into a squad car, and driven away. She was still watching as the crowd gathered in somber knots, Joe's father in the middle, and moved off.

"I know who can help us," she said slowly.

"Emmy!" Brian looked nervously at the door. "Listen, my uncle might come back any minute."

With a zipping sound and a tiny grunt, two heads poked out from Emmy's backpack—one gray and furry, and one with a thatch of rumpled yellow hair.

Brian's mouth hung open for a full minute.

"I think I'd better tell you everything," said Emmy.

She sat down on the couch and went through it all. It sounded even more impossible when she said it out loud.

"So does this kind of thing happen often?" Emmy asked earnestly. "I mean, your back room is full of rats with tags that say they can do amazing things—"

"Back room?" said the Rat alertly. "Full of rats?"

Brian looked puzzled. "Listen, why does this rat keep squeaking? Does he think he can talk or something?"

The Rat looked annoyed. "What's his problem? Wax in the ears?" he muttered and slid off the couch. "I might just check out these rats in the back room."

"I don't want to see any more rats," said Joe. "Just unshrink me, is all I ask."

Brian looked worried. "I don't really know how," he began, when the phone shrilled.

"The Antique Rat, may I help you?" said Brian. "Oh—hello, Uncle, I've been worried. You're *where?* JAIL?" He glanced at Emmy. "Um hmm . . . uh huh . . . just a minute." He opened the desk drawer and pulled out a pen and a piece of paper.

"Okay, I'm ready now—shoot. Um hmm . . . uh huh . . . in the blue case? No—okay—I see it."

Brian scribbled down notes industriously. Joe, bored, began to do flips on the sofa cushion. Emmy leaned back and shut her eyes.

She wasn't worried. Brian would never give them away, she knew, and maybe he could figure out how to fix everything. It was a relief to let someone else do the thinking, for a change. She was so tired . . .

"Emmy! Wake up, I've got to go."

Emmy opened her eyes as Brian shook her shoulder. "Huh? Go where?"

Brian looked at the paper in his hand. "I've got a delivery to make to the old Addison place. And then I've got to find my uncle a lawyer."

"The old Addison place? That's my house!" Emmy sat upright. "You can give me a ride home."

"But what about me?" Joe stood on the middle sofa cushion, looking very small.

Brian looked thoughtful. "Could you just go home with Emmy tonight? In the meantime, I can look around. Professor Vole has lots of notes and things. I'll see if I can find directions for . . . for unshrinking—"

"SISSY!" shrieked the Rat from behind the velvet curtain. "I'VE FOUND YOU AT LAST!"

The Rat's short furry arms clutched the Shrinking Rat of Schenectady through the metal bars of her cage. The two rodents, their gray fur damp with tears, looked identical except for the white patches behind opposite ears.

"Torn from the nest," sobbed the Rat brokenly, his words half muffled in the other rat's shoulder. "I never thought I'd see you again, my own dear Sissy."

"That explains why she looks so much like Ratty," Emmy whispered to Joe, who was perched on her shoulder. "She's his sister! Do you suppose she can shrink people, too?"

"Come on, if you want a ride," Brian urged, poking his head into the back room. "I'm late."

The Rat leaped from the bank of cages to Emmy's shoulder, nearly knocking Joe off. "You've got to set Sissy free!" the Rat cried, but Brian was already striding out the door, a blue carrying case in his hand.

Brian's truck was old, loud, and rusty. Emmy, bouncing in the front seat, held Joe carefully. The Rat scrambled up to the driver's headrest and perched there, shouting in Brian's ear.

"Why can't you let Sissy go?" the Rat demanded indignantly. "What has she done to you?"

Brian changed gears with a clashing noise. "What's he saying?"

Emmy repeated the Rat's words.

"Sorry," he yelled over the roar of the truck's engine. "My uncle left me in charge. I can't just start letting the rats go, they're his *business*."

"Have a heart!" the Rat cried. "She's been in a cage for *years*! Your uncle has no right—"

"Give it a rest, Ratty, he can't understand you," said Emmy. "I don't know why."

Brian accelerated over a series of potholes, and the Rat's voice cut off abruptly. He hung on to the headrest with all four paws.

"Joe! You okay?" Emmy asked.

"S . . . sort of." Joe hung on to her thumb, looking sick. "Are we almost there?"

Emmy looked out the window. "Yes—I see my house. There's Jems, driving out—"

She gasped. She had forgotten! With everything that had happened, she had forgotten. It was six o'clock, and Jems was driving to the airport to pick up her parents. She could see his taillights glowing at the end of the block.

Emmy stared out the window, unblinking. She had missed meeting her parents, the best part of all, and now she had to face Miss Barmy. Who knew what the nanny might do to punish her for being late and skipping gymnastics . . . she might not get to see her parents at all tonight. She sat in silent misery, a dull weight in her chest.

"Here we are!" said Brian cheerfully. "And there's that mean lady, waiting at the back door. Emmy?" He bent over and peered at her beneath the dashboard. "Why are you hiding?"

"I can't face her yet. I've got to think up a story."

"Who? The mean—" Brian looked embarrassed. "Sorry, is she your mom or something?"

"No, my nanny, and she's *horrible*—"

"All right, just stay there if you want. I've got to make the delivery, though."

Brian grabbed the blue carrying case out of the back and went up the walk, whistling. Miss Barmy stepped out.

"You're *late.*" Miss Barmy's voice was murderous.

Emmy, under the dashboard, flinched.

"Sorry, ma'am. My uncle couldn't come himself, but I thought you'd want your delivery anyway."

There was a silence. "You thought correctly, young man. However, I am most *seriously* displeased, and I shall speak to your uncle about it. Give me the case."

Emmy looked at Joe, whose tiny face looked as puzzled as she felt.

"Yes, ma'am. I'll come to pick it up in two hours."

"Make it three," snapped Miss Barmy. "And when you come back, park that noisy truck a block away and walk."

The back door slammed. Brian got into the truck and wiped his forehead. "Whew!" he said. "She's your nanny?"

"Yeah, worse luck," said Emmy gloomily. "Brian— what, exactly, did you deliver?"

"Some rat," Brian said. "My uncle had it all ready in the carrying case."

"But what is she going to use it for?"

"Your guess is as good as mine." Brian started the truck. "I don't use 'em, I just deliver 'em."

"Wait." Joe tugged at Emmy's sleeve. "Aren't we getting out here?"

Emmy nodded. "I've got to find out what she's doing with that rat. Will you help me?"

"I'll do anything, as long as I don't have to ride in this truck anymore. I'm about to lose my lunch."

"I'm coming, too!" The Rat leaped onto Emmy's backpack as she slipped out of the truck and ran for the bushes.

Emmy balanced carefully on an overturned bucket that the gardener had left out.

"Careful," said Joe, crouching in her palm as Emmy lifted him over her head. "Don't tip so much. Up a little more . . ." He stepped off her hand onto the kitchen windowsill.

The Rat scurried up a woody vine that clung to the stone.

"Can you see anything?" Emmy whispered.

"I see a mixing bowl, and, um, part of a stove. . . ." Joe pressed his small face to the glass.

Emmy leaned against the stone wall. "Do you see Miss Barmy anywhere?"

"Yeah," said Joe. "She's rolling something around with her hands on the counter."

"Rolling? Like a ball?"

"Yeah, like a big—a big ball of—"

"She's kneading dough, you dim bulb," said the Rat. "Don't you know anything about baking?"

"Oh, like you do," said Joe. "Seriously, I liked you better when you *didn't* talk."

"Well, if you would ever *read* . . . *Nummi Gourmet* always has a whole section on breads, it's *basic*—"

"Rat," said Emmy sternly, "*shut up.* Joe, can you see the carrier?"

"Yes . . . yes, there it is. She's opening it up now, she's taking out this big bushy rat—"

"It's a *chinchilla*, brainiac," muttered the Rat.

"What's she doing now?" Emmy fidgeted on the bucket.

"Okay, um—she's got the chinchilla, and—oh my gosh!"

"*What?*" Emmy straightened. "I can't see anything! What's she doing?" She grabbed the ledge and stood on her tiptoes. The bucket teetered.

CRASH! Emmy fell through the shrubs. BANG! The bucket spun out and hit the side of the house.

"Ow!" cried Emmy as she landed, scraping an elbow. Too late, she clapped a hand to her mouth.

Above her, Joe and the Rat peered down from the windowsill.

And then, with a creak, the door opened. A metal-tipped shoe poked out. Emmy held her breath.

10

HONK! HONK HONK!

A yellow cab rolled up the driveway. The back door opened before the driver had time to set the brake, and Emmy's parents spilled out, laughing and talking all at once.

"Emmy! Sweetheart, did you fall? Are you hurt?"

"Here's my girl!" Emmy's father reached her first and lifted her high. "You've grown! Keep that up and you'll be playing basketball!"

Emmy laughed, almost giddy with joy. She was really too big to be lifted in the air by her father anymore, but she didn't care. It felt absolutely wonderful.

"I get to hold her, too," Emmy's mother protested, and then they were all three hugging, Emmy in the middle and a parent on each side. Emmy was breathless by the time they set her down, but it didn't matter. "Did you have a good trip?" she asked, beaming. "Are you going to stay home now?"

Metal-tipped shoes came tapping down the back steps. "Welcome back, Mr. and Mrs. Addison," said Miss Barmy, fluffing her hair and smiling her tight-lipped smile. "I'm dreadfully sorry you had to take a cab—I *did* send Jems with the car. Was your plane early?"

"Nope, five thirty, right on time." Emmy's father nodded to the driver, who took the bags out of the trunk. "Jems wasn't waiting, so we just took a cab. No harm done."

Emmy glanced up quickly. So she had been right about her parents' arrival time, and Miss Barmy had been wrong! And after all that fuss in Dr. Leander's office, and having to swallow that stupid vitamin drink!

Emmy almost laughed. If she had come home at the time Miss Barmy said, and had ridden with Jems, she'd be sitting at the airport right now while her parents were home with the nanny.

Or was that what Miss Barmy had planned all along?

Miss Barmy came a step closer. "Emmaline has just had a fall. Perhaps she should lie down and rest."

Emmy's father looked at his daughter, who was shaking her head vigorously, and laughed. "She doesn't look tired." He patted Miss Barmy on the shoulder. "We appreciate your concern, though. It's clear that Emmy is healthy and happy, and that's the important thing."

He wheeled around, looking up at the imposing stone house, the gnarled trees overhead, and threw an arm over his wife's shoulder. "It's great to be back, isn't it, Kathy? Why did we ever leave in the first place?"

"I haven't the faintest idea," Kathy Addison said cheerfully, brushing Emmy's hair back from her face. "We must have been out of our minds. Let's go inside, sweetheart. I want to hear all about school and everything else."

Emmy turned to go in with her parents. But as she looked back over her shoulder, she saw that a muscle had begun to jump in Miss Barmy's cheek.

"And then I got an A+ on this project, 'Animals of India.'"

Emmy, seated on the leather couch between her mother and father, was enjoying their undivided attention. From time to time she'd reach into her binder and pull out more papers, and they admired and asked questions about every one.

Just now her father was looking through her math workbook, nodding approvingly and checking her answers. Kathy Addison was deep into Emmy's latest book report, curled up against the sofa arm, her light brown hair falling forward against her cheek. Emmy leaned back, full of contentment.

The view outside the window was spectacular. A soft breeze moved fitfully through the big, graceful elms, making dappled and moving shadows on the wide, green lawn. Out on the lake, bright sails moved back and forth in Loon's Bay.

It wasn't quite like the old days, when they had all lived in the little apartment above the bookstore that Emmy's parents had owned. The view, in those days, was of a scraggly tree and a busy street. They hadn't had any leather couches, and their one carpet had been faded and threadbare.

Emmy pressed her feet into the thick Oriental rug and looked around at the gleaming grand piano, the fresh flowers in polished vases, the crystal chandelier. It was all very nice. Very, very nice, but—it just wasn't very important. What *was* important was sitting on either side of her, and that, at least, was just like the old days.

Emmy leaned against her father's shoulder. "Dad? Are you going to get the sailboat out this weekend?"

Jim Addison studied the lake. "I don't see why not. The water's a little cold, but the air is warm enough . . . oh, Jems, there you are!"

Jems was standing in the doorway, chauffeur's cap in hand. "I'm sorry, sir," he said in his dignified way. "I was told the wrong time to pick you up. I should have checked on it myself, sir."

"No problem," said Emmy's father, getting up. "Say, Jems, I'd like to get the sailboat in the water tomorrow. Are you free after breakfast?"

Emmy's eyes widened as she watched Jems walk to meet her father. Clinging to the chauffeur's trousers, with his back paws anchored on one well-shined shoe, was the Rat—and hanging on to the other cuff was what looked like a blond action figure in a blue jersey.

She had forgotten all about Joe and the Rat, stuck on the windowsill. They must have climbed down the vine, but what were they doing hanging off Jems's pants leg?

"Mom?" she said quickly. "Here are more reports to read, when you're done with that one." She added to her mother's stack, watching her eyes.

"Mmm," said Kathy Addison absently, turning over a page. Emmy relaxed inwardly and glanced back at the chauffeur's ankles—but Joe and the Rat were gone.

"*Psst! Don't eat them!*"

Emmy jerked her head around and saw the Rat sliding down the back of the sofa.

There was a small but decided tug on her socks. Emmy bent over as if to look in the backpack she had left on the floor—the rat pee had dried by now—and found herself staring at Joe's tiny, worried face.

"Listen, Emmy—don't eat them! And don't let your parents eat them!"

"Eat *what*?" Emmy whispered. She glanced up through her bangs as Miss Barmy's cane tapped into the room.

Behind her, Mrs. Brecksniff held a silver tray in her hands. And on the tray was a coffee service, with cups, plates, jam, butter, and—

"Grandmother's potato rolls!" announced Miss Barmy.

Emmy's mother looked up. "Oh, Miss Barmy, you shouldn't have."

Jim Addison chuckled. "It would hardly feel like coming home if we didn't get those rolls, Miss B. You must have made them for us after every single trip we've taken."

"I know they're old-fashioned," said Miss Barmy sweetly, "but there's nothing like the taste of bread made by loving hands."

Mrs. Brecksniff, closely followed by her cat, set the tray on the coffee table with a thump. Muffy meowed, looking attentively at the tray.

"Sit down, Miss Barmy; you should at least enjoy the rolls with us."

"Of course," said Miss Barmy. "I should be honored to join you during Emmaline's quality time." She seated herself on a wing chair, crossing her legs at the ankles.

Emmy felt cold. It was like watching a cobra rising, getting ready to strike. *What* was in those rolls?

Muffy rubbed against her leg, purring. Emmy ignored her.

It didn't matter what was in the rolls. She just had to get rid of them. But how?

The cat meowed, sounding muffled. Emmy looked down. Muffy had her head *right in the backpack* . . .

"Muffy, no!" Emmy shot off the sofa and grabbed the cat by the hind legs.

Muffy dug in her claws, looking bored. Emmy dragged her out. Relieved to see that the cat hadn't gotten Joe or the Rat, she was about to let her go—and then she had it. Her solution.

She pinched the cat.

"*Mrrrrraaoow!*"

Hissing, spitting, and furious, Muffy twisted violently in Emmy's hands. Emmy, pretending to struggle for control, waited until the perfect moment—the perfect trajectory—and let the cat go, just like a bomb over a target.

"Oh! Oh no! My *potato rolls!*"

The coffee was spilled. Miss Barmy was on her feet. And the potato rolls were everywhere—on the floor, behind the couch, under the table . . . one had even shot across the room and landed at Jems's feet.

"Oh, gosh," said Emmy. "I'm so sorry."

"You—you're *sorry*—" Miss Barmy gripped her cane with both hands, her knuckles white over the little carved faces.

"Maybe we could just dust the rolls off and eat them anyway," suggested Emmy's father.

"Jim," said Kathy Addison, sounding amused. "The cat *landed* on them."

"Ah well, we'll have to get along without them this once. It's too bad, Miss B."

"Maybe I could help you bake some new ones?" Emmy said brightly.

"Thank you, that won't be necessary," said Miss Barmy, her voice icily controlled. "I shall bake new rolls myself. This very moment."

"I absolutely forbid it." Kathy Addison's voice was firm. "You've made us feel very welcome, Miss Barmy, but I insist that you take the rest of the evening off. We're going to—" She looked at her husband.

"We're going to take Emmy out for burgers and malts," said Jim Addison promptly. "Run on up and drop off your things, kiddo. We're going on a picnic."

Emmy grabbed her backpack, hoping devoutly that both the Rat and Joe were in it by now, and waved at everyone on her way out of the room. She waved especially hard at Miss Barmy, whose eye had begun to twitch.

11

"If i never see the inside of your backpack again, I can die happy," said Joe, staggering out onto Emmy's floor.

"You and me both," muttered the Rat.

"And I had no idea a cat's teeth were so *big*!" Joe shook his head.

"That was no cat—that was an Assassin."

"An Executioner."

"A Furball with Homicidal Tendencies."

"*Will* you two listen?" Emmy opened the door to her playroom. "I'm going out for a while. Why don't you guys just hang out in here? There's a dollhouse, and little cars, and an electric train . . . you might find something warmer to wear, Joe; not Barbie clothes, either."

"Sure, Emmy. After you, Your Rattiness."

"No, after *you*, Dandelion Head."

"Lead the way, Sir Fuzzalot."

"Arrrrrgh! I'm leaving!" said Emmy.

"What's wrong with her, Teenyboy?" said the Rat, scampering toward the playroom door.

"No idea, Shaggy Guy," said Joe, tearing after him.

"Hey, wait! What *was* in those rolls, anyway?" Emmy called.

"Tell you later!" shouted the Rat.

"You're safe for now, Emmy!" Joe's voice came faintly. "Hey, cool, Ratty, look at the train!"

"Seriously, Jim—why do we do it?" Kathy Addison, seated on a bench by her husband, looked out over the bay.

They had brought take-out food down to the beach. Talking, laughing, skipping stones across the water . . . it had all been as wonderful as Emmy had ever hoped for. But now, lying on a blanket a few feet away from her parents, she pretended to be absorbed in making patterns in the sand. Grown-ups always talked more if they thought you weren't listening.

"Why *do* we travel all the time? Was it really necessary to attend Count Whaposki's polka stomp, and the anniversary of Princess Rotunda's liposuction? And how about that German guy, what was his name?"

"Baron Kartoffelpuffen von Shtinken?"

"Yeah, him. Be honest, now—did you *really* enjoy the Five-Day Sauerkraut Fest and Hedgehog Hunt?"

"Well, the little fellows *were* pretty cute when they rolled up, all spiny—"

"I thought so. And what about the week on the yacht with that billionaire and his very bouncy friend?"

"Bimbo LaRue? The starlet who only knew words of one syllable?"

"That's the one. Jim, what do we have in common with people like that, after all?"

"Not one thing, except . . ."

"Except money," Kathy Addison finished.

There was a pause. "Well, would you want to go back to living above the bookstore and pinching every penny?" her husband demanded.

"That wasn't such a bad life. We had fun together, we had work we believed in, and we had Emmy. Your great-uncle William may have left us his estate, but that didn't mean we had to give up everything else we loved. Sometimes I wish he had left it all to those other distant relatives . . . his second cousins once removed, or first cousins twice removed, or what-ever they were . . . he didn't even *know* us."

"We haven't given up everything else we love!" Jim Addison raised his voice. "Emmy? Come here, honey, I want to ask you a question."

Emmy got up. "Yes, Dad?"

"Listen, kiddo." He pulled her to his knee. "Do you remember the bookstore Mom and I tried to run? Do you remember how tough it was?"

"It was fun," Emmy said promptly. "We ate dinner together every night, and then we'd read together in the big blue chair. And on weekends you'd let me help in the bookstore, too."

"You see?" said Emmy's mother.

"I remember that blue chair." Emmy's father sounded disgusted. "It was worn through on the arms and the back left leg kept falling off."

"It was the best chair in the world," said Emmy sturdily.

Emmy's father looked at his wife.

"Told you so," she said. "Emmy knows what's important."

Jim Addison grinned. "I know when I'm beat." He got up and shook out the picnic blanket. "Bedtime for you, Emmy. But why don't we read a story or two tonight?"

"Let's!" said Emmy's mother. "We don't have the big blue chair anymore—"

"That's a relief," muttered Emmy's father.

"—but, Emmy, you can bring your pillow and some books to our room, and we'll all pile onto the big bed and read. How does that sound?"

"Great!" said Emmy, starting to skip.

"And tomorrow afternoon," added her father, "once Jems and I get the boat ready, we can go sailing."

"Jim, we have a charity function at the house tomorrow, remember? It's already on the calendar, so we can't cancel it now."

"All right, we'll get the boat ready Saturday morning, and put it in the water in the afternoon."

"And can we go to church together on Sunday?" asked Emmy. "Maggie goes. And we used to."

Emmy's mother nodded. "I can't remember the last time we sat in a pew together," she said thoughtfully. "See, Jim, I told you Emmy knows what's important."

"Point taken," said Emmy's father, starting the car. "But if you say 'I told you so' one more time, I'm calling Bimbo."

Emmy danced up the stairs to her bedroom. What book should she pick? A new story or an old favorite? She rummaged through her pajama drawer and found some fuzzy blue ones. Perfect. It would remind Mom and Dad of the chair.

"Hey, guys!" Emmy poked her head into the playroom. "I brought you some supper."

They had forgotten to shut off the electric train. Emmy flicked the switch on the control box and the hum from the motor abruptly died.

"Ratty? Joe?"

There was a soft grumbling rattle from somewhere near her feet. Emmy knelt to look in the dollhouse and there was the Rat, snoring in a miniature bed.

"Ratty? Where's Joe?"

"Snurrrgh," said the Rat and rolled over. "Snorrk."

"Joe? Are you there?"

Joe's head emerged from a third-story window. "Did you bring me any supper?"

Emmy handed him the bits she had saved in her napkin. "Listen, Joe—what was in the potato rolls? What did Miss Barmy *do* with the chinchilla?"

130

Joe swallowed a bite of french fry. "She made a bunch of little dough balls, for the rolls, you know . . ."

Emmy nodded.

"Then she grabbed this chinchilla around the middle and made it stick out one of its feet. And then—in every roll—she stamped it!"

Emmy felt sick. "She stamped a *rat's* foot? In the *rolls?*"

"Yeah, and she didn't wash it first either. Was she trying to poison you guys or something?"

Emmy knelt on the floor, perfectly still. She was thinking back to the little room full of cages in Professor Vole's store. Back to the tags, each with a special power, each with its own instructions.

She didn't remember seeing the chinchilla, and she had no idea what its tag had said. But there was *some* kind of power that Miss Barmy had hoped to use on the Addison family, and odds were it wasn't anything good.

There was a knock on her door. "Come in," Emmy called, and Maggie entered, carrying a plate of milk and cookies.

"Wow." Emmy looked at the chocolate wafers with crème filling. "What's the occasion?"

"Miss Barmy insisted on sending up snacks." Maggie, smiling, set the plate down on Emmy's bedside table. "Better hurry, now. Your parents are waiting."

Maggie whisked out. Emmy stared at the plate. And then slowly, carefully, with a slight twisting motion, she lifted the top wafer off one of the cookies.

There, slightly blurred in the crème filling, was the imprint of a rat's foot.

Emmy grabbed a book at random and headed for her parents' bedroom. It was going to be complicated to explain, but once her parents saw the rat print in her cookie—well, they'd *have* to get rid of Miss Barmy.

Emmy gave a little skip of joy as she opened her parents' door—and stopped. The book slipped from her fingers.

"Look at this closet! Just *look* at it!" Kathy Addison wailed. "I have absolutely *nothing* to wear, we're having *people* over tomorrow, and I don't have *time* to fly to New York. . . ."

Emmy stepped behind her mother and looked anxiously at the closet bulging with clothes. "How about this one?" She pointed to a pale green silk. "You wore that to the orchestra gala, didn't you?"

"*Exactly.* I wore it two months ago, I couldn't *possibly* wear it again. One of my friends would be sure to notice."

"But—" Emmy hesitated. "If they're your friends, they wouldn't make you feel bad about it, would they?"

"Oh, darling, you are *so* naïve. Friends are the *worst;* they'll rip you apart, you can't let your guard down for a single *minute.*"

Emmy swallowed hard and looked around the room. Her father, hunched over on the edge of the bed, was talking fast on the phone. She turned back to the closet and tried again. "This pink one is pretty, Mom . . ."

"That's not *pink,* darling, what a plebeian name, it's *brine shrimp*—but the color is *so* last year. There's no hope for it, I'll just have to get hold of Carravacci in New York tomorrow, and God only knows if I'll be able to find anything *decent,* much less the right *shoes.*"

"Don't give me that load of horse puckey!" Jim Addison's face got redder as he yelled into the phone. "You can get me a direct flight if you try. Name your price—you can bet I'm not hanging around in Frostbite Falls for any three hours while some minimum-wage dolt finds an excuse to lose my luggage."

"Dad?" Emmy tugged timidly at his sleeve. "Weren't you going to read with me?"

Her father ruffled her hair and looked at his watch. "Not tonight, baby, Daddy's got some very important business to take care of."

"But, Dad, you promised . . ."

"I know, honey, and I really *want* to, but you *know* how important these recreational opportunities are to me, I've been so busy and I really need to get away. . . ."

Emmy's voice was very small. "Are you going away tomorrow?"

"No, baby, we're going to have the whole weekend together, just like we planned. I'm not leaving until Monday, that is, if this cretin on the phone ever gets his act together— What?" Emmy's father spoke into the phone. "You can get a direct flight to Alaska Saturday night? That's great, that's fabulous, book it."

He banged down the receiver and smiled broadly at Emmy. "There you go, doll, we'll have all day tomorrow and most of Saturday, too. You can't ask for more than that!"

He picked up the phone again. "Jack? Jim Addison here. I'm going to need the best salmon-fishing outfit you've got. . . ."

Emmy sat on the edge of the bed without moving, a small, miserable lump in blue fuzzy pajamas. Slowly, painfully, she looked at her father. He had forgotten her completely.

Emmy stood up stiffly. There was no point in staying here any longer. She stooped at the door to pick up the book she had dropped—and then she saw it.

A tray, on a little table. Two mugs of tea, half drunk . . . and a plate with a few broken fragments of cookies still left on it. Sandwich cookies with crème filling.

Emmy stared at the plate and then at her parents, so suddenly changed. She saw it all—*now* she understood.

There was a soft thumping down the hall: Miss Barmy's cane. Emmy, feeling hot with anger and sick with fear, turned to face her.

"Bedtime, Emmaline," said Miss Barmy, her eyes glittering with triumph. "Quality time is *over*."

12

"So what do you think the chinchilla's powers actually are?" Joe, seated cross-legged on Emmy's bed, had found some action-figure clothes and was toying absently with the dog tags around his neck.

"The power to make my parents crazy? At least *I* didn't eat her filthy cookies. . . ." Emmy picked at her bedspread, frowning. "But I've eaten Miss Barmy's potato rolls before and nothing much happened to me."

Joe looked up. "You're sure? You've eaten the same kind before?"

Emmy nodded. "They didn't have any effect on me. Or— Wait!" She shut her eyes, trying to concentrate. "I do remember times when I didn't exactly feel like myself. All mixed up, sort of, and I'd get really interested in—oh, I don't know—stuff I usually didn't care about. Like I remember one day I woke up and there were fifty Barbie outfits in a bag on my dresser. I remembered shopping for them, I remembered wanting them like crazy, and then later, I couldn't figure out why. I don't even *play* with Barbies."

The Rat cleared his throat. "Fascinating though the subject of Barbies may be, don't you think we should get back to what's really important? The rat man is still after me, you know. And we *have* to release Sissy."

"*You're* what's important?" said Joe hotly. "What about me being the size of a chipmunk? Or the Barmster trying to turn Emmy's parents into zombies? Doesn't *that* bother you?"

Emmy jumped in quickly. "Listen, guys, it's *all* important. But we can't go chasing off, trying to rescue Sissy or anything, because we don't know enough yet."

"You've got *that* right," said Joe. "I've got about a million questions. Like, was it really the Rat's bite that shrank me? And if it was, how come I didn't shrink when he bit me once before?"

"How can we rescue Sissy?" added the Rat, pacing over the bedspread, his claws leaving little holes.

"I've been wondering why Miss Barmy hates me so much," Emmy said. "And why she wants this weird power over my parents."

"Here's another one," said Joe. "Why does she have to keep using the chinchilla? Does it wear off?"

Emmy sat up abruptly. "Hey, I guess it must!"

"Don't sit up so fast," cried the Rat, landing on his ear.

Emmy ignored him. "It's got to wear off, or Miss Barmy wouldn't have to keep baking more potato rolls every time my parents come home from a trip!"

"Ow!" Joe did an involuntary somersault. "Look, stop bouncing, will you?"

"Sorry." Emmy made an effort to keep still, but she was too excited. "See, this has all happened before. My parents come home, and they're happy to see me, and everything is just like it used to be. And then pretty soon, sometimes just a few minutes later, it's like they hardly know I'm around. Only this time it took a couple of hours—"

"Because you dropped the cat on the potato buns—nice work, by the way—"

Emmy nodded. "So the rolls do their work long enough for my parents to leave town again, but by the time they get back, it's worn off. That's one thing we know for sure—the chinchilla's power doesn't last." She hesitated, remembering with a sinking

139

feeling that her parents' trips had been getting longer and longer. Did that mean the chinchilla poison was building up in their systems? Might there come a time when it *wouldn't* wear off?

"Hey!" Joe looked bright eyed. "Maybe shrinking doesn't last, either!"

"I've probably got more staying power than a *chinchilla*," the Rat muttered.

"Let's hope not," said Emmy. "Because we still don't know how to unshrink Joe if it doesn't wear off. With any luck, Brian's found—" She stopped abruptly.

"What?" said the Rat. "Cat got your tongue?"

"Hush!" Emmy whispered fiercely. From the other side of the bedroom door came the sound of scratching and then a plaintive "*meow!*"

The Rat clawed frantically across the bedspread. "It's the Assassin!" he gasped, huddling as close to Emmy as he could get.

"No, Ratty, not the *cat*—listen! Outside—can you hear it?"

A soft night breeze swirled past the curtains. The high, rhythmic sound of spring peepers filled the room. And then a low, throbbing rumble came distantly to their ears.

The rumble coughed, rattled, and died.

"That's Brian's truck," said Joe, listening intently. "He's come back to pick up the chinchilla, and he's parking a block away, like the Barmster told him to. Do you suppose he's found directions for unshrinking me yet?"

"Let's find out." Emmy grabbed her robe. "I hope you guys don't mind riding in the pockets. There's one for each of you, and they're nice and soft."

They were safely down two flights of stairs when the dramatic voice of a newscaster rolled out from the den.

"And in other news today, a human tragedy is unfolding in the town of Grayson Lake—"

Emmy stopped at the doorway and listened.

"—yes, little Joe Benson was brutally abducted today in broad daylight—"

"*Little?*" protested Joe from Emmy's left pocket.

"Shhh—you're little *now,* anyway." Emmy opened the door a crack.

"—and police have taken a local resident, Professor Cheswick Vole, into custody. Professor Vole apparently threatened the boy earlier today, accusing him of stealing a classroom pet—"

"*Cheswick?*" snickered the Rat.

The newscaster, a man with a long jaw and thick hair, kept talking as a photo of Joe was shown. Emmy pushed open the door. Her father was watching the news, reading the paper, and sending an e-mail all at once.

"Dad? Mind if I watch the news with you?"

Jim Addison grunted. "Just don't bother me, I'm busy."

"—and Monica Blapper, our Channel 82 studio reporter, has unearthed some interesting facts about the professor."

"That's right." Monica Blapper patted a stray hair into place and fixed the camera with a serious gaze. "Cheswick Vole grew up right here in Grayson Lake, a boy like any other."

A picture of some high school kids flashed on the screen, a circle highlighting a thin, small boy with glasses.

Emmy blinked. Who was that girl behind him? She looked familiar.

"—and so he left his hometown for New York to study with the famous Maxwell Capybara, world-renowned professor of rodentia. Now, tragically, he is implicated in the disappearance of Joe Benson—"

Emmy felt an impatient movement in her right pocket. "What?" she whispered, distracted.

The Rat tugged at the pocket's edge. "Let's go! We'll miss Brian!"

"We go now to the sobbing parents and Studley Jackell, on the scene. Studley, are you there?"

"Yes, Monica. Mr. and Mrs. Benson, would you like to share your heartbreak and pain with our Channel 82 viewers tonight?"

The camera switched to a close-up of the Bensons' front entryway. Studley Jackell seemed to be struggling for position as someone from inside tried to shut the door.

"Just give us a few brief words," begged the reporter through the slowly narrowing gap. "Let it all out, Mr. and Mrs. Benson, as our viewers peek into the innermost depths of your soul. . . ."

Joe's father thrust his head through the Bensons' front door. "I'll give you a few words," he roared, his face crimson. "GET OFF MY PROPERTY, YOU VULTURES!"

The door slammed. Studley Jackell turned toward the camera and dabbed at his eyes. "Well, Monica, as you can see, the parents are nearly crazed with grief—"

"You go, Dad!" murmured a voice from Emmy's left pocket.

Emmy put her finger to her lips, glancing at her father, but he was deeply absorbed in the stock market listings.

"—but even more crazed is the bizarre Professor Vole, as you can see from this video, taped by an alert bystander today in front of Grayson Lake Elementary."

The screen was suddenly filled with the enraged face of Brian's uncle, yelling on the street as police handcuffed him, "I want my rights! I want my rat!"

"This is Studley Jackell—"

"—and Monica Blapper, wishing you a good evening from Channel 82, where We Care About You,

We Share About You, We Lay Every Detail Bare About You."

Emmy quietly closed the door and backed into the hallway.

"Wow," whispered Joe.

THE KITCHEN WAS DARK. Emmy padded across the tiled floor, creaked open the back door, and poked her head out into the cool night air.

"Brian?" she said cautiously.

The Rat bumped against her hip as he shifted restlessly. "I can't get comfortable," he muttered peevishly. "It's too cramped in here."

Emmy ignored him. The night was full of sounds—the sigh of a lake breeze through the elms, the soft slap of waves on the shore. Somewhere, a door slammed. A dog barked. And then came the sound of footsteps—but they weren't Brian's, and they weren't outside.

The kitchen light flickered on. Emmy whirled. "Miss Barmy!"

The nanny, carrying a blue plastic case, blinked in the sudden light. "Well, Emmaline?" She slid the case behind the counter.

"I was just getting some fresh air—"

Miss Barmy's eyes narrowed. "Don't lie to me, Emmaline. Clearly you must have a nutritional imbalance of staggering proportions." She paused, her lips thinning. "You dropped that cat on my potato rolls on purpose, didn't you?"

"I wanted a drink of water, too," Emmy went on, edging sideways to the sink.

Miss Barmy took a step closer, fixing Emmy with a menacing stare. "What were you doing this afternoon by the back door?" She bent over Emmy like a hawk over its prey. "And why were you late coming home from gymnastics?"

Emmy swallowed nervously and reached for a glass.

"You're hiding something, aren't you?" Miss Barmy smiled coldly. "Come, Emmaline. Tell Nanny everything."

Emmy, desperate, gripped the glass in both hands—and then she remembered. Miss Barmy, too, had something to hide!

"I really came down to see the truck, Miss Barmy." Emmy opened her eyes wide. "Didn't you hear it?"

Miss Barmy paled.

"That same truck was here this afternoon." Emmy cocked her head, frowning. "Why, I wonder?"

A footstep scraped outside. Miss Barmy jumped.

Emmy tried for a serious, worried expression. "Who could be coming to the back door at this time of night? I'd better get my dad."

The nanny looked suddenly sick. "No, that won't be necessary, Emmaline—"

There was a knock—three soft, insistent raps.

Miss Barmy's hand descended on Emmy's shoulder and propelled her across the kitchen floor, out into the hall, and halfway up the stairs. "We'll say no more about it, Emmaline. Now run up to bed."

The nanny gave Emmy a last little shove, hurried down the steps, and shut the door of the kitchen behind her with a solid click.

"Mean old witch," said the Rat.

Emmy looked thoughtfully at the drinking glass, still in her hand. She had seen something in a movie once. . . . Would it work? She tiptoed down the stairs.

"What are you going to do?" asked Joe, poking his head out of her pocket.

"Shhh," Emmy whispered, slipping into the linen closet beside the kitchen. She closed the door behind her, and in the darkness she set the open end of the glass against the wall and pressed her ear to the bottom.

"You didn't bring the full order!" Miss Barmy's voice came clearly through the glass.

"I . . . I'm sorry, I'll tell my uncle." Brian's voice was fainter, as if he was turned away. There was a slight scraping noise, and a soft chittering that could have been the chinchilla.

"But why isn't Cheswick attending to this personally?" There was a tapping sound, as of an impatient foot.

There was a pause. "He's in jail, ma'am. Would you like to sign this receipt?"

"The fool! He's going to ruin everything I've worked for!"

Brian cleared his throat. "He should be out soon; maybe even tonight. The lawyer is working on it—"

"Give Cheswick a message for me, young man." Miss Barmy's voice was menacing. "The chinchilla was good enough for tonight, but I need the school order—the usual—by *tomorrow*. Whenever he comes back—anytime, I don't care if it's in the middle of the night—have him call me. Do you understand?"

"Call you. Middle of the night. Yes, ma'am," said Brian, his voice fading.

The back door slammed. Miss Barmy and her cane stumped past the closet, up two flights of stairs, and down a hallway before Emmy cracked open the closet door.

"We still have to talk to Brian," said Joe worriedly.

"Right." Emmy stared up the stairs. "But how about when Miss Barmy's asleep? Say, midnight?"

The clock in the hall struck twelve.

"Wake *up*, Ratty!" Emmy reached into the dollhouse and shook the plump gray body.

"I tried shaking already," said Joe, rummaging through a pile of doll's clothes by the soft glow of the nightlight.

The Rat, sprawled across a four-poster bed, snored gently. His hind leg was tangled in a blue flowered comforter, and a thin line of drool showed at the corner of his mouth.

"We can't leave him here alone." Emmy gazed at the Rat with a mixture of fondness and irritation.

"He'd scare Mrs. Brecksniff, or get caught by the cat, or bite someone."

"Yeah, and they might shrink or they might not," said Joe, pulling out a blue sweatshirt. "Criminy, this is small."

"That one's for Ken's little brother; try this." Emmy pulled out a green army sweater with G.I. Joe insignia. "What do you mean, they might not shrink? Oh wait, that's right—"

"The first time he bit me, nothing happened, remember?" Joe thrust his head blindly into the sweater. "The other day, when I fed him a carrot—"

Emmy laughed. "And he told you off yesterday after school and you couldn't believe he could talk."

"Hey! That's it!" Joe's face emerged from the neckhole, flushed and triumphant. "First time he bites you, you can understand Rat speech—"

Emmy gasped. "That's why I could understand him all year . . . he bit me on the first day of school! And the second time the Rat bites you, you shrink—"

"And the third time? What happens the third time he bites you?"

Emmy stared at Joe. "I don't think I want to know."

Joe grinned. "Maybe you disappear!"

"What, you think that's funny?" Emmy was appalled.

"I don't mean gone for good, I just mean invisible. Face it, Emmy, that would be *so* cool."

"Maybe—as long as you knew how to get visible again." Her voice was muffled as she pulled on a sweatshirt.

"And get back to normal size. I sure hope Brian's found out how to unshrink me."

"He's got to have some instructions somewhere, for all those rats. Here, I'm just going to put the Rat in, bed and all."

"Put some toys in, too, to keep him busy when he wakes up. But *I'm* not riding in that thing. It still stinks."

"Where, then? In my pocket?" Emmy scooped a handful of doll's toys and a tiny red wagon into her backpack and carefully placed the Rat on top, tucking the comforter around him.

"No, I'll ride in your sweatshirt hood. Just pull the drawstring tight, so I don't fall out."

Emmy slipped down the stairs and out the back door as silently as she could. "Drat you, Muffy!" The cat was already through her legs and behind the hedge.

Emmy stepped out across the lawn. The moon was high, but the shadows it cast were so dark they looked solid. The grass, wet with dew, made her socks soggy around her ankles, and Emmy breathed in the fragrant, cool air. It was oddly exciting to be out so late, with no adult knowing where she was or what she was doing.

She groped along the footpath with one hand outstretched, and then her feet found the solid asphalt of the street. Up the hill, and a left turn on Main: it was the same path she took every day to school, only wonderful and mysterious by night.

"Are we there yet?" Joe's voice sounded faint from inside her hood. "I'm suffocating in here. Let me out, will you?"

They were almost at the alley. Emmy carefully shrugged off her backpack with the sleeping Rat still inside and set it on the sidewalk. Then she sat down on the front steps of the art gallery and gently slid down until the hood of her sweatshirt rested on the top step.

Joe clambered out and breathed deeply, stretching to his full four inches of height. "This brick looks a lot smoother from higher up," he muttered, stumbling on the uneven surface.

Emmy, hot from her walk, pulled off her sweatshirt, dropped it by the backpack, and leaned back on her elbows. The moon shone on the roof of the school across the road and etched the playground equipment with silver light. Emmy wondered where the soccer games were played, the rodent games that Ratty had watched with such longing from his cage.

Joe leaned on her shoulder, staring at the schoolyard. "It looks lonely, like nobody ever played there, or had any fun at recess."

"I never did," said Emmy.

"You never had fun at recess? Why not?"

Emmy shrugged. "It's hard to have much fun by yourself." She tossed a bit of gravel onto the street. "At my old school I had friends just like anybody else. And it's not like the kids here are mean to me. It's just that they don't seem to see me at all."

"Well . . ." Joe's voice was thoughtful. "I didn't notice you myself for a long time. And then all of a sudden I did. And—it was weird, the way even Mr. Herbifore kept forgetting your name. I mean, you were so *good* and all. Mostly teachers pay a lot of attention to the good kids."

"He remembered my name today, though. And that girl who sits in front of me actually said something to me, for once."

"Yeah, well, the Barmster hasn't been around for a while, poisoning everybody's minds against you."

Emmy sat up straight. "What did you say?"

Joe sounded confused. "It was just a joke. I didn't mean she really poisoned us. I mean, all the treats she brought us were wrapped, and straight from the store."

"She actually came to the school? With treats?"

Joe stared at her. "Weren't you there? She'd come maybe twice a month with a basket of treats, and this scented candle that smelled sort of weird, during—"

"During silent reading," Emmy finished, seeing again in her mind's eye the pink envelope on Mr. Herbifore's desk containing the mysterious note written in Miss Barmy's elegant script. Now it made sense.

"I never knew," Emmy said bitterly, "because twice a month Miss Barmy made me go see that nutty Dr. Leander and talk about my so-called problems. And all the while it was because she wanted to come to my class behind my back."

Joe gave a low whistle. "So she wanted you out of the way while she messed with our heads. Maybe another chinchilla print in the cookies, or maybe something funny in that smelly candle . . ."

"And it made me practically invisible to everyone in that whole class."

Joe chewed on his fingernail. "But I don't get it. Why wouldn't she want you to have any friends?"

"Because she's mean, that's why." Emmy was boiling.

"Well, yeah, but she's got to have another reason,

or why would she go to all the bother? She can be mean to you in lots of ways."

"I don't know." Emmy put her chin in her hands and glared down at the sidewalk. "I'm tired of trying to figure things out, and I'm sick of that disgusting Miss Barm—"

She stopped abruptly, gazing at the thin, oblong patch of light that stretched for a few inches along the sidewalk. It came from a crumbly sort of hole at the base of the steps. "Look," she whispered, pointing.

Joe flopped down on his stomach to peer over the top step. "So? Someone must have left the light on in the gallery basement, and there's a crack in the foundation."

Emmy squatted on the sidewalk, staring at the tiny glow. It hadn't been there before, she was almost sure. She reached out a tentative finger—and whipped around, knocking over her backpack. Something warm and furry had brushed her arm.

"*Muffy!* You scared me to death!"

The cat rubbed up against her, purring in a self-satisfied way. And then the Rat screamed.

"Where am I? I smell a cat! *Mommy!*"

"Oh, gosh . . ." Emmy reached inside the backpack to comfort him. "Ratty, it's just Muffy, I'll protect you—"

"The big hand! *The big hand!* I'll *bite* you, I will—"

"Ratty! *No!*" Emmy yanked her hand away, but the sudden, sharp pain in her finger told her it was too late. She had been bitten—twice.

14

IT WAS, EMMY THOUGHT, a telescoping kind of experience. She had, first, an odd, shrinking feeling in her stomach, very like going suddenly down on a fast elevator. Next came a prickling in her arms and legs. And last came the intensely strange sensation of watching her sweatshirt and backpack grow mountainous above her.

There was a long silence.

"Now you've done it, Ratty," came Joe's voice from the top of the steps.

"I didn't mean to," sobbed the Rat. "Don't blame me, I have nightmares."

Emmy sat flat on the sidewalk, her legs the size of chalk sticks. Any minute now, she'd wake up. Any minute now . . .

"*Meow?*" Muffy padded closer.

Emmy's heart gave a great panicked jolt as the sharp, predatory scent of cat filled her nose. She risked one horrified look upward and felt her insides go soggy. Those cat teeth—so huge! And that pink tongue that licked all around as Muffy yawned, wide as a cave!

Emmy didn't even want to think about the claws, or the way that Muffy played with a mouse, batting it back and forth until the poor thing died of terror. Instinctively, she crawled into her sweatshirt and down the sleeve. The air was stifling, but it beat being eaten alive by Muffy, the Assassin.

"Hey! Muffball! Get lost!" Joe's voice, sharp with anxiety, pierced through the cotton surrounding Emmy's ears. "Ratty, help!"

A low, frightened moan came from the depths of the backpack.

"SCAT!" shouted Joe, and a small, fierce burst of gravel skittered across the sidewalk.

"*Mrrroouw!*" snarled Muffy.

"Don't antagonize her!" begged the Rat. "Run and hide, that's the rodent's way!"

"Not when a friend is about to be eaten, it's not," hollered Joe, and another tiny handful of gravel pattered down.

Shakily, Emmy worked her way out of the sweatshirt. Her heart was thundering in her ears, but she couldn't let Joe fight the cat all alone. She emerged from the sleeve and yelled, but all Muffy's attention was on the small creature who was pelting her with stinging bits of rock. The cat leaped lightly onto the brick stairs.

"Joe!" Emmy shouted, aghast. "Run!"

Joe whipped his head around. On either side of him was a drop of five steps. Behind him was the closed door to the art gallery—and before him, advancing with what looked like murderous intent, was Muffy.

"Remember the rodent's creed!" the Rat called, peering out from the backpack with quivering whiskers. "Find a hole and *hide!*"

Joe hesitated, then leaped straight for the cat.

The Rat squealed. "And *through* the front paws and *under* the belly, Joe Benson makes a diving roll—and he's *down* one step, what a leap that was, ladies and gentlemen . . . and now he's hanging by his fingers, he's—yes—no—*yes*, he does a drop and bounce to the next step down, this is simply amazing, what form, what style—and he throws in a foot fake! The cat looks confused—no mouse has ever scampered quite like this before—"

"Go! Go!" whispered Emmy, clenching her fists so tightly that her nails dug into her palms. "You can do it, Joe! *Go on!*"

She was yelling now, cheering as Joe scrambled from step to step, dodging and cutting back as if he were in a soccer game with no ball. Muffy, behind him, bobbed her head from side to side in an attempt to follow his erratic progress.

Emmy clapped her hands together with relief as Joe disappeared into the crumbling hole under the brick steps, momentarily blocking the thin gleam of light that still shone from within.

"He makes it!" cried the Rat in triumph. "And the score stands at 1–0 with the Muffster pouncing just one second too late!"

"Shut *up*, Ratty!" Emmy whispered hoarsely. But it was too late. Muffy, abandoning the hole in the brick, made one bound and whipped out a paw just as the Rat turned to run.

"Help!" the Rat squeaked. "She's got my tail!"

"No!" Emmy shouted. "*Bad Muffy!*"

Muffy turned, yellow cat eyes gleaming. But just then there came a small clatter from the hole in the steps, and a subdued sound of voices.

Emmy stared. Emerging from the hole was a miniature wooden tower on wheels with a pole sticking out the back. The pole had a leather basket on one end and a twisted rubber band on the other, and pushing the whole contraption were two rodents.

They were fuzzier than the Rat, and their fur looked reddish in the streetlight's glow. As they stood on their haunches to adjust the levers on their machine, Emmy could see two slender stripes of dark fur all down their backs and tails. They were chipmunks, and they were wearing work gloves.

"Steady there, Chippy," said the larger one. "Turn 'er one more notch. What's the trajectory?"

"Lessee," mumbled the smaller chipmunk. "Distance to feline one point seven meters, height of ears twenty centimeters, gravitational pull constant . . ."

Emmy glanced at the cat, who appeared fascinated.

". . . cat at zero velocity. Initial cocklebur speed four point three meters per second . . ."

"Hey," interrupted the larger chipmunk, "that cat isn't going to stay at zero velocity forever. How about my method? Aim, then fling?"

"But, Buck!" Chippy's voice was anguished. "I haven't even calculated the coefficient of drag on the cocklebur! It's got an uneven surface! It's going to spin!"

"Do your best, Chippy. Now—ready, aim—"

"Fire catapult!"

With a *fwing!* the catapult whizzed forward, pitching a prickly-looking ball in a perfect arc. Muffy, unable to decide between attacking the Rat or the chipmunks, held still one moment too long—and got the cocklebur squarely in the ear.

"Mrrreeeeoowww!"

"Slam-bang on target. Reload, Chippy, we'll go for another shot!"

"She's turning, Buck—bump her over another ten degrees—"

Fwinggg!

"YOW Yow yow yow *yow yow yow!*" Muffy's cries, piercing at first, grew faint as she disappeared into the distance.

Buck and Chippy fell over each other, laughing.

"Now *that's* what I call a sensitive spot!"

"I didn't calculate for *that* target, Buck, but if she's going to run with her tail in the air . . ."

"Yep, that cat's going to have a little coefficient of drag on her behind for a while—"

Chippy hooted, holding his stomach. "Oooh—stop, I can't breathe—"

Buck chuckled, tied back the catapult, and wheeled it around.

"Can I help?" Joe hovered nearby.

"Well, you can introduce us to your friends. Mother wants everyone to come in for refreshments."

"All right, boys, cocoa's almost ready. Go on and watch the kettle so it doesn't boil."

The voice was kind but firm. A no-nonsense sort of voice, Emmy decided as she watched a round, furry rodent emerge from the hole beneath the steps and march straight toward Emmy's gigantic sweatshirt.

"Child?" The chipmunk peered around a sleeve. "Don't be afraid, dear, it's just Mrs. Bunjee. Come along and we'll have a nice cup of hot chocolate and get you to bed. Humans are daytime animals, I know, and it's far too late for a child like you to be out, what with cats on the prowl and who knows what else . . . why, what's the matter?"

"I can't go to bed," Emmy explained wearily. "It's going to be a long walk to Brian's now that my legs are so short. Then I have to find out how to stop

Miss Barmy, and get my parents back, and unshrink Joe, and free Sissy—"

"Why, you poor thing!" Mrs. Bunjee's stubby arm was around Emmy's shoulders. "You're all worn out, and no wonder! The first thing to do," she went on in a decided tone, "is come have a little something. And then we'll talk. Because we're all going to help you, of course. You're too young to carry these worries all alone."

Something inside Emmy welled up and spilled over at the kindly words, and she buried her face in Mrs. Bunjee's soft, furry shoulder.

"There, there," soothed Mrs. Bunjee, patting her on the back. "Go ahead and cry, it won't hurt you a bit."

"I'm all right now," gulped Emmy, rubbing a sleeve across her eyes. She had gotten a bit of fur up her nose and she wanted to sneeze.

"Of course you are. Now, come along with me and you'll feel better in no time." Mrs. Bunjee scrambled over the sweatshirt sleeve and trotted on ahead.

The sidewalk was not nearly so smooth as it looked from several feet up, and Emmy stumbled as she hurried after Mrs. Bunjee. But she hesitated as she came to the crumbling hole.

Mrs. Bunjee popped her head out again and grasped Emmy's hand with a firm paw. "Come along, dear. Step *around* the crack, watch your head through the passageway, and—here we are!"

Emmy emerged from the dimly lit tunnel, blinking. Over her head the ceiling was low and rough, but beneath her feet was a smooth wooden walkway, neatly joined, and just ahead was an opening where Joe stood in front of a polished railing, his back to her. Beyond him was light, and movement, and a sense of space.

Emmy wedged herself in beside Joe and gasped. She didn't know exactly what she had expected—something cramped and earthy, perhaps—but she had never imagined *this*.

She was in a city, an underground city, with walls of warm red brick and rough wooden beams. Festoons of clear Christmas lights twinkled along every brace, joist, and beam, and swooped in bright curves down to the floor far below. Twiggy ladders led to platforms of all sizes, lofts that stuck out from supporting posts like perches in a complicated sort of tree. And peering out from every loft, and leaping from ladder to ladder, and swinging across vast spaces on thick knotted ropes were rodents of every kind. Chipmunks and rats, gophers and mice, tiny brown voles and big gray squirrels, and they all seemed to be chattering at once.

"Can you *believe* this?" Joe leaned over the railing. "They must have tapped into the electricity."

"They've dug out so much space," Emmy said, dazed. "How did they ever do it? And how did they build all these lofts and things, and"—she leaned over the railing—"are those actually railroad tracks down there?"

"This must be the crawl space," Joe said, calculating on his fingers. "Yeah—probably only about four feet deep or so."

"But it feels so high up! There must be six levels beneath us!"

"That's about right. We're only a few inches high, you know. Four feet, to us, is going to seem like being on top of a six-story building. Hey, Ratty, see any cousins?"

Emmy looked at the Rat. He was standing a little ways off, his eyes glazed. "Finally," he murmured, pressing a paw to his heart. "*These* rodents will appreciate an educated Rat. They'll elect me mayor, no doubt. I shall have to prepare my acceptance speech. 'My dear little friends . . .' No, too patronizing. 'My fellow rodents . . .' Yes, yes, much better."

The Rat wandered along the walkway that encircled the city, muttering to himself. Emmy looked at Joe, dismayed, but Mrs. Bunjee's firm paws urged them forward. "Come, my dears. Trot along, that's right, third loft on your left."

They hurried along the walkway to a twiggy-looking loft tastefully adorned with fresh spring leaves and violets, and through the garlanded door to a comfortable-looking kitchen with big cushiony chairs, a kettle on the hearth, and a table set out with steaming mugs.

"There, now!" Mrs. Bunjee clapped her paws together. "Sit down and help yourself. Buckram, Chipster, will one of you run out and ask Professor Capybara if he would stop by? Try to keep him calm. We'll need his help, I think."

Emmy glanced at Mrs. Bunjee over the top of her mug. Professor Capybara—now why did that name sound familiar?

"I'll get him," said Buck, heaving himself upright. "Chippy's working on the pawball roster. We're playing on the gophers' home field tonight, and if they beat us again, I won't be able to show my face above-ground for a week."

"What's pawball?" asked Joe.

"It is a rodent sport," said an authoritative voice from the doorway. The Rat entered the chipmunks' loft and surveyed them grandly, in the manner of a teacher about to explain a difficult subject. "I have watched it often through my schoolroom window. Played with a small leather ball—"

There was a sudden clatter as Mrs. Bunjee dropped her mug. "Oh my!" She stepped closer to the Rat and sniffed deeply. "Raston? Raston, is it really you?"

15

"RASTON? WHO'S RASTON?" The Rat looked over his shoulder.

"I think she means you, Ratty," whispered Emmy.

The Rat drew himself up to his full height. "You must have mistaken me for someone else, madam. I know no chipmunks."

"Nonsense," said Mrs. Bunjee. "You used to tumble about with chipmunks all the time. Don't you remember?"

"*I?*" said the Rat, frostily. "Tumble about? With *chipmunks?*"

"I know you by your smell, you see," said Mrs. Bunjee, smiling.

"Smell?" The Rat drew back, offended. "I do not smell, madam. I washed, I brushed, and I even used Summer Breeze hair gel!"

"Hair gel," muttered Chippy, shaking his head over the pawball roster. "That explains it."

"I could not possibly be mistaken," said Mrs. Bunjee firmly. "Still, to be absolutely sure . . ."

She put a paw on his shoulder and bent back the Rat's left ear. The small, triangular patch of white showed up clearly in the lamplight.

"Dear, dear Raston," she said, grasping his paws between her own. "I knew your mother when you were just a little ratling in the nest. And I saw when you were taken—you and dear Cecilia—and then, a moment later, the big hand grabbed me, too."

The Rat collapsed into a vacant chair. "Mommy," he whimpered. "What happened to Mommy?"

"She came back to the nest to find you gone, and it broke her heart, I imagine," Mrs. Bunjee said briskly. "Sit up, Raston; show some backbone. Drink your cocoa, it'll put heart into you."

Emmy set down her mug, licked the foam from her lips, and leaned her head back against the chair cushions. If Buck didn't get back soon with this professor person, she'd go find him herself. It was long after midnight, and they had to get going . . . she had to talk to Brian right away. She had to stop Miss Barmy. She would just . . . close her eyes . . . for one minute more. . . .

Voices filtered into Emmy's consciousness like sounds dimly heard underwater. She stirred, stretched, and poked her head out from beneath the blanket someone had tucked around her. It was a soft tan, with two white stripes edged with black. She looked at it for a moment, dazed, as she tried to remember where she was. Across the table, Joe was talking.

"So that's pretty much the story, sir. Brian was going to try to find some directions for unshrinking us. We were on our way to his place. He lives on the second floor of the Antique Rat with his uncle."

"Ah." There was a pause, and the sound of a match striking, then a scent of something burning, more fragrant than tobacco. "This uncle. What does he look like?"

"Skinny," said Joe immediately, "with a beaky nose. Clothes too big for him. Going bald."

There was a sound of steady puffing. "By any chance, do you remember his name?"

Joe hesitated. "Charles? Chester?"

"Cheswick," said Emmy, suddenly awake. "Professor Cheswick Vole."

She stared at the gentleman sitting across from

Joe—a man about as big as a well-fed squirrel, with half-glasses on his nose, a white beard, and a pipe in his mouth.

"*Professor* Vole!" snorted the gentleman. "*He* was never a professor. He was just a lab assistant. He stole my rodents, and he stole my research! All my notes . . . endless years of work—"

"Steady, Professor, dear," said Mrs. Bunjee worriedly, patting his shoulder. "Don't get excited, now."

The professor shut his eyes and took a series of deep breaths. The red in his neck began to fade.

"But where did you get the rodents in the first place?" asked Joe.

"I found them all over the world." Professor Capybara opened his eyes and placed his fingertips together, looking almost calm again. "They were rodents whose ancestors had been captured long ago, when certain tribes had noticed some special power the rats had, and over time had learned how to use it. I merely took them from cages in the jungle, or desert, or savanna, and put them in cages in the laboratory. I assure you, they were well fed and treated with the utmost care."

"But of course," said Mrs. Bunjee gently, "we were still *caged*. Emmy, dear, now that you're awake, I'd like you to meet our own Professor Maxwell Capybara."

"Delighted," said the professor, smiling from under his bushy eyebrows.

Emmy took in a breath. "Now I remember! They said your name on the news, when they arrested Prof—I mean, Cheswick Vole! You were his teacher! The professor of rodentia from New York!"

Emmy shook the professor's hand warmly. Everything would be all right now. The professor would find his notes and research at the Antique Rat. He would unshrink everyone first, of course, and then he would explain about all the rat powers. There had to be at least one rodent in the back room that could stop Miss Barmy once and for all.

"But if you bought the rodents already caged, who captured Ratty, then?" Joe persisted.

"The big hand!" cried the Rat, starting awake. "Mommy! Sissy!"

Professor Capybara knelt beside the Rat. "My dear Raston," he said quietly. "Cheswick Vole took you from your nest without my knowledge. But it was I who taught him how to recognize rodents of power, and so I share in the blame."

The Rat blinked.

"I have paid for it since," the professor went on humbly. "I was asleep in the lab—I sometimes take rather sudden naps, you see—when Cheswick Vole made sure you bit me twice. When I shrank, he caged me along with the rodents and drove us far away."

The Rat shivered. "I remember that trip," he said plaintively. "It was dark, inside a big box. And I got sick to my stomach."

Professor Capybara nodded. "When he stopped for the night, I unlocked my cage. I tried to open all the others, too, but he came back too soon. Only about half the rodents escaped. Unfortunately, your sister was not among them."

"Sissy!" moaned Raston, his eyes moist.

"Those of us who were free scattered, hiding miserably under bushes and in holes and cracks in the walls, cold and wet and frightened."

"I remember! I remember shivering on the playground, all alone!"

The professor looked sorrowful. "I never saw you, Raston. The next morning, you must have been picked up by Emmy's teacher."

"And put in a cage, and given disgusting food in little pellets, and forced to listen to a bunch of slow learners for *years*!"

Professor Capybara looked at the Rat sternly. "At least you were warm and dry and safe. We had a terrible first year, trying to survive. But little by little, we worked together to create a community. The rats had their powers, and I, in turn, taught them everything I knew of science and philosophy and engineering."

"That explains the electricity," said Joe under his breath. "And the city."

"But now that I know," the professor went on, his neck getting pinker, "now that I know Cheswick Vole did not drive away from this place, as I had thought . . ." He got up and began to pace. "Now that I know he lives just a block away, in this very town—"

"Remember, Professor!" cried Mrs. Bunjee. "Breathe—go to your happy place—"

"What will you do? WHAT WILL YOU DO?" screamed the Rat, jumping up and down.

"DO?" shouted Professor Capybara. "I'm going to—" He stopped, swayed, and put a hand to his eyes. "I believe I'm going to take a little nap," he said faintly, went limp, and hit the floor.

16

THE NIGHT AIR WAS fresh and scented with lilacs.
On the sidewalk outside Rodent City, Emmy's backpack still lay on its side.

"All clear," said the Rat alertly.

Emmy and Joe dashed for the pack, jumped into
the opening, and rummaged around in the dark.
"Ow!" said Emmy, bumping her shin on the four-
poster bed. "Help me push this out of the way, will
you?"

The bed slid out onto the sidewalk, followed by a
little yellow truck and a doll-sized high chair.

"How many toys did you put in here?" said Joe.
"Wait, here it is."

"Don't push yet," Emmy said. "Something's caught
in the wheel—okay, here we go."

Emmy grabbed the handle and Joe pushed from
behind, and a small red wagon rattled across the
graveled sidewalk and stopped at the crack beneath
the gallery steps.

"All right, boys!" called Mrs. Bunjee, and Buck and Chippy came staggering through the gap, carrying the professor between them.

"He's a deadweight when he's like this," said Chippy, breathing hard.

"It's a good warmup for pawball, though," said Buck as they wedged Professor Capybara into the wagon. His feet dangled almost to the ground, but he looked more comfortable once Mrs. Bunjee tucked a small, flowered pillow from the four-poster bed beneath his head.

Emmy glanced around quickly for any lurking cats. "Will he wake up by the time we get to the Antique Rat, do you think?"

"Perhaps," said Mrs. Bunjee, "or it might take a bit longer. But the minute he wakes up, he'll be on the spot to help. Come, child, out of the way—here comes the pawball team."

A rumbling of paws sounded in the tunnel passage, and a pack of rodents in red and white jerseys streamed from the crumbling hole in the foundation. The Rat cheered loudly, waving both paws. "I can't play the first quarter," he cried, "but do your best, lads, and I'll come as soon as I can!"

Buck looked at him blankly as Emmy and Joe stifled giggles.

"Nice-looking jerseys," said Raston breezily. "Where's mine?"

Buck scowled. "Listen here, you're *not*—"

"Come on!" called Mrs. Bunjee. "Run along behind them; there's safety in numbers," and they all grabbed a bit of the wagon and pushed hard to catch up.

"But I still don't understand about Professor Capybara," said Emmy as they trotted down the dark and echoing alley. "Why does he fall asleep so fast?"

"Ratolepsy," said Buck briefly.

"It's a rodent-induced sleep disorder," Chippy added as they skirted the garbage cans, even smellier at ground level.

"You get it from the Bushy-Tailed Snoozer Rat," Mrs. Bunjee explained. "Years ago, the professor examined one too closely and it sneezed in his face. He came down with the Snoozer virus, and—well— he hasn't yet found a cure."

"So whenever he gets excited, he gets sleepy?" Joe looked down at the professor, whose peaceful face was lit by the streetlight as they emerged from the alley.

"More like comatose," said Buck.

"Out cold," said Chippy.

"It never lasts long, though," said Mrs. Bunjee. "Sometimes just a few minutes, but never more than an hour—why, Professor! You're awake already!"

"Here's what I've got so far." Brian yawned as he helped Emmy, Joe, Raston, and the professor get settled on a large wooden desk near the window. "I couldn't get into the cabinet—he keeps it locked—but I found lots of his papers."

They were inside the Antique Rat. The chipmunks had run off to the pawball field while the Rat had swarmed up the vine-covered brick to ring the doorbell. About fifty rings later, a rumpled-looking Brian had come to the door. Although he was surprised to see that Emmy, too, had shrunk, he let them in, was introduced to the professor, and set them on the desk amid a stack of old books and papers.

"Wonderful! All my old notes!" Professor Capybara adjusted his tiny glasses, sat down in the circle of light cast by the desk lamp, and heaved open the first of the notebooks. "Hee hee! Here's the experiment with the Spiny Pocket Mouse—dear me, that one went badly awry; I couldn't sit down for a week. And the Dog-Eared Marmot! What a charming rodent, except for its unfortunate habit of barking at night . . ."

Emmy glanced at Joe. "Professor," she said uneasily, "that's all very interesting, but could you possibly look up the directions for unshrinking us first? If I'm not my normal size by morning, Miss Barmy will—" She hesitated. She didn't know exactly what Miss Barmy would do, but she could just about guarantee it would be bad.

"Oh, of course. Let's see. We were doing shrinking experiments in the spring of the year, as I recall . . . but which year?"

Joe wandered over the desktop, jumping from book to book to read the titles, but the Rat tugged at Brian's sleeve. "I want to get Sissy out of her cage."

"Eh?" Brian looked down. "Why is he squeaking at me again? I can't understand a thing he—*yeeouch!*"

The Rat stepped back from Brian's forearm with a satisfied air. "Can you understand me now, mate?"

Brian stared down at the drop of blood welling from the puncture. "Yeah," he muttered. "Thanks. Sort of."

"I'll go with you," Emmy said. She might as well be doing something instead of just sitting around watching the professor think.

The back room was as Emmy remembered it—only more so. The smells were more overpowering, the teeth of the beaver more frighteningly orange, and the cages seemed to stretch on forever.

Brian dialed the combination to Sissy's cage and let Raston in. Emmy was touched to see the Rat patting his sleeping sister gently on the shoulder.

"Sissy? It's me, Raston—your brother—"

"Rasty?" Cecilia sat up and threw her arms around her brother. "I knew you'd come back!"

"Dearest Sissy," murmured the Rat, his voice breaking with emotion.

Emmy caught sight of the Endear Mouse as Brian turned away. "Wait! Can I go in there?"

Brian looked confused. "Do you know that mouse?"

"Sort of," said Emmy, remembering how she had put out a finger and the Endear Mouse had touched it with its small, white paw.

Brian dialed another combination and opened the door. Emmy stepped off his hand and into the cage of the tiny mouse with its beautiful fawn-colored fur and serious brown eyes.

"Do you remember me?" she asked softly.

The little mouse smiled, its dark eyes lighting, and patted the floor of the cage.

"Do you—want me to sit down?" Emmy asked.

The mouse nodded and patted the floor again. It watched her expectantly.

Emmy walked over, kicking up wood shavings, and sneezed. She sat down beside the Endear Mouse, and the lovely fur, as soft and light as thistledown, brushed her arm for a moment. Its touch was strangely comforting.

Emmy had never forgotten the words printed on the tag of white pasteboard: "Endear Mouse. Makes the absent heart grown fonder." If only she could somehow use the mouse's powers now, she wouldn't have to wait for the chinchilla effect to wear off. She wouldn't be at Miss Barmy's mercy for weeks more while her parents were off on another one of their trips.

She fidgeted, wondering if the Endear Mouse could speak. The mouse sat quietly, white paws folded. Its ears, too large for the little face, looked ready to listen.

And suddenly Emmy was ready to talk.

She told the mouse about the early days, when they had owned the bookstore on the other side of town, before her great-great-uncle William had left them all the money and the house on Grayson Lake—how her parents had loved her, then.

Emmy's voice grew colder as she talked about Miss Barmy—how the nanny had been waiting at the door of the big house, how she had invited them in as if she owned the place, serving them tea and Grandmother Barmy's potato rolls. Miss Barmy said she had known Great-Uncle William well, and she had been nanny to many children over the years; and she could tell just by looking at her that Emmy was a *good* girl.

Emmy stood up and walked to the bars of the cage, looking out. "She showed us her cane, carved with all these little faces. She said they were the faces of people she had taken care of. And all at once I got this horrible, creepy feeling. Only she was smiling, and my parents were smiling, and everybody thought everything was wonderful, so I didn't know what to think."

She turned and told the rest of it—how people at school barely knew she existed, how her parents had changed, and how it all—every bit of it—could be traced to Miss Barmy.

"She's ruining my life," Emmy said bitterly. "I've got to stop her. I just don't know how."

The Endear Mouse made a sudden movement, its face stern.

"What? What are you saying?" Emmy watched as the mouse made a fierce, stabbing gesture with its paw.

"You're saying . . . I should fight?"

The mouse nodded vigorously.

"Of course, but—with a sword?" Emmy was dubious.

The mouse smacked a paw on its own forehead, then pointed to Emmy's with the other paw.

Emmy looked at the mouse, feeling stupid. "I'm sorry, I don't get it—"

Stepping forward, the mouse took Emmy's face between its own two paws and pulled it down until their foreheads touched.

All at once Emmy understood. "You're saying we should fight her with our minds! Working together!"

The mouse broke into a wide smile, its eyes crinkling with delight.

"So you'll help me?" Emmy cried happily.

The Endear Mouse put its paws over its chest and bowed. But its eyes, when it raised its head again, were deeply sad.

There was a noise of feet, and a swish as the curtain to the back room was pulled aside.

"Emmy?" Brian stopped before the cage and peered in, his nose astonishingly huge to Emmy's eyes. "I think you should come. The professor's having some trouble."

Professor Capybara looked up anxiously, surrounded by papers yellowed with age and covered with neat, precise handwriting. "I can't seem to find anything, my dear. Cheswick must have been messing about with my notes—they're all out of order, and I just can't remember—" He blinked rapidly, looking upset.

"Stay calm, Professor," said Emmy, patting his shoulder in her best imitation of Mrs. Bunjee. "Doesn't Ratty's sister have something to do with the unshrinking part? I mean, her tag said—"

"Yes, yes—we know that much already." The professor flipped through the scattered pages in a helpless manner. "The question is how, exactly, does she do it?"

Sissy scampered up the desk leg behind Raston. "How do I do what?" She waved shyly at Joe and Emmy.

"Why don't you try some experiments?" Emmy suggested. "Eat something with her paw print in it, maybe."

"I've got some leftovers from lunch," Brian said, pulling out a brown bag.

"Psst—Emmy," said Joe, beckoning from behind a large book.

"Hang on." Emmy watched as Sissy stepped on a peanut-butter sandwich, imprinting her foot in the soft, white center. The professor ate it hurriedly.

"Is it working? Am I growing yet?" he asked, looking down at his arms and legs. "If this doesn't work, we'll try something else." He scribbled awkwardly with a pencil stub, as large as a baseball bat in his hands.

Emmy sighed internally. Professor Capybara might be a brilliant rodentologist, but he seemed a little dense sometimes. "Brian could take notes for you, Professor," she said politely. "He's big enough to hold the pencil, you see."

"Why, of course! What a splendid idea, my dear!"

Emmy walked across the desk blotter to Joe. "What's up?"

"Look—it's Cheswick Vole's old high school yearbook. Check out the hair!"

Emmy leaned over the glossy page with sudden interest. "Hey, that's the picture they showed on TV."

Joe nodded, studying the group photo. "Old Cheswick could have used a weight-lifting class. That boy was the classic ninety-eight-pound weakling."

Emmy knelt on the page for a closer look—and took in a sudden breath.

"What?"

Emmy pointed, her hand wavering slightly.

"But, Emmy, it's just the names of the kids. Cheswick Vole, Priscilla Addison, Peter Peebles, Jane Barm—"

They stared at each other.

"Wow," said Joe, turning back to the photo. "She could have been a model."

Emmy nodded. Jane Barmy, at seventeen, *was* beautiful, but her face already seemed hard and a little mean. "She looks like the type who pinches when the teacher's back is turned," Emmy said with quiet scorn.

There was a grunt of pain from the professor, who was holding his finger. Cecilia, looking embarrassed, was wiping blood off her front teeth.

"What do you think? Am I growing?" the professor asked eagerly.

The Rat shook his head. He and Sissy stood in the circle of lamplight, their fur tipped with gold. Brian, still in his pajamas, made a notation on a pad of paper.

The clock on the wall ticked loudly in the silence, and Emmy glanced at it. Almost two in the morning, and no solution in sight. At this rate, she'd still be chipmunk-size when Maggie called her for breakfast.

She suppressed an internal quiver of impatience. She had thought the professor would know exactly how to fix things, but it wasn't working out that way at all.

Well, she would just have a look at those notes herself. She walked around to the other side of the pile, picked up the nearest paper, and read: "Genetic mutations from two RATZ intercrosses (HRRY × RT and RAT × FZZY)."

Emmy swallowed hard and reached for another paper. "Intergenic rodent recombination in phage

191

T12," she read. " 'Mutagenicity of mouselike compounds.' 'Snoozer Bacteriophage SNZ.' Well, that's helpful," she muttered, letting the papers fall.

"Emmy," said Joe abruptly. "Look here."

He had turned the pages of the yearbook back to the beginning. There, under the Bs, was Jane Barmy's senior picture—surrounded by little hearts drawn with a red marker.

Emmy looked at Joe in disbelief. Cheswick Vole loved *Jane Barmy*?

"That's why he lets her use any rat she wants," Joe said, grinning. "At least the ones he's figured out how to use."

"And he never charges her anything," said Emmy sourly.

"Of course not. He's in loooove!" Joe pretended to swoon.

Emmy turned away. How anyone, even Cheswick Vole, could love someone as poisonous as Miss Barmy, she didn't know. Who cared if Miss Barmy was good-looking? She was as ugly as could be on the inside.

"Please, no!" Cecilia's voice rose. "I've nipped your finger and stomped on your food and everything else you could think of. I couldn't bear to claw your face! There is a limit!"

"But—" began the professor.

"Anyway, how do you know I'm the one who can unshrink you?" she pleaded. "Maybe it's Raston who can do it!"

The professor shook his head. "Raston shrinks, you enlarge. That's why you're a pair. You did it to a cat once, in the laboratory. Don't you remember?"

"I remember that cat," said Cecilia gloomily. "Sensitive— always getting its feelings hurt. But I have no idea how I made it grow."

"Don't you think you could have scratched it," the professor said persuasively, "by accident?"

Cecilia looked thoughtful. "Maybe."

"Well, then. One more try?"

Cecilia sighed and swiped his cheek with a quick claw.

"Ow!" Professor Capybara dabbed at the cut with his hanky, looking anxiously down at his body. "Am I growing yet? Can you see me growing? Anyone?"

They all waited. And waited.

"I knew it," said Cecilia unhappily. "Now you're bleeding again." Impulsively, she leaned forward and kissed the professor on the cheek she had scratched. And then, all of a sudden, she tumbled backward, because—

"Ouch!" the professor said, astonished, as he bumped his head on the ceiling. He climbed down off the table, laughing and excited. "My dear, dear Cecilia! How very clever of you! And it makes sense, yes indeed. A kiss is the opposite of a bite, you might say!" He pulled Brian from the chair and improvised a polka, dancing with short, awkward leaps. "Hooray for Cecilia! Hooray for science and the experimental method! Hoo—hoora—"

The professor wavered, buckled, and went down in a heap.

Brian backed away, appalled.

"Criminy," said Joe. "Not again."

"But he wasn't even mad—he was *happy*!" Inwardly fuming, Emmy climbed down the drawer pulls, hand over hand, and ran up to the professor's large and hairy ear. "Wake up, Professor! We still need you to help us figure out the potions—and what to do with the rats—and Miss Barmy—"

She stopped. Footsteps sounded outside the shop, and there was a rattling of keys.

Brian spun around. "Quick! Hide!"

He dragged Professor Capybara behind a large, locked cabinet, then sprawled in the chair again, shutting his eyes. Joe took refuge behind the stack of yearbooks. The rodents swarmed down the desk to the floor, running with Emmy to a shadowy corner.

The door creaked open. A man entered.

He was small and shabby, with thinning brown hair and trousers belted high. He dropped his keys into his pocket and looked up. "Brian!" Cheswick Vole rasped, sounding suspicious. "What are you doing up?"

"Huh?" Brian jolted upright and shook his head as if to clear it. "I've got a message for you, Uncle. From that Barmy lady."

Cheswick's eyes brightened. "Jane sent me a message?"

Brian nodded. "She said to call her as soon as you got back, day or night, it didn't matter."

Cheswick cracked his knuckles one after the other, smiling dreamily. "She needs me! She misses me!" He picked up the phone on the desk and began to dial.

The Rat and Sissy clung to each other as Cheswick's feet came nearer. Emmy patted their furry backs while her eyes watched Cheswick's every move. She couldn't afford to panic—she had to think.

"Go to bed, boy," Cheswick snapped. "This is a private conversation."

Brian moved slowly in the direction of the stairs.

"Jane? Jane, it's Chessie . . ."

A voice squawked loudly. The happy glow faded from Cheswick's face.

"I'm sorry—but you said 'the usual'—"

There was a pause, then more squawking.

"Yes, yes, of course," Cheswick said hurriedly. "I'll get it ready right away. You can come anytime, anytime at all . . ." He looked at the receiver. A dial tone droned loudly into the silence.

"Well . . ." Cheswick set the phone down and wiped his palms on his trousers. "Let's see. Extract of Gerbil, triple distilled, and Scent of Shrew. I think I have those bottles already made up."

He shuffled over to the tall cabinet, fumbling with his keys, and unlocked the door. The clink of bottles followed, and then, faintly, the sound of a snore.

Cheswick's back stiffened. He put a vial back in its place and peered around the edge of the cabinet. His face turned the color of putty.

"Professor? Boss?" he whispered.

Professor Capybara's chest rose and fell in peaceful rhythm. A slight whistling sound exuded from his nose.

Cheswick smiled slowly: a big, bony smile. He moved his hand delicately among the bottles in the cabinet, selected one, and measured out three drops. He bent over the professor.

Deep in the shadows, Emmy gave the Rat a sudden shove. "Go on, Ratty—bite him."

17

"NOOOooo!" cried Cheswick as he shrank, down, down, until he was face to face with the Rat.

Raston showed all his teeth in a wide, sinister smile.

"Brian!" Cheswick called, his voice a thin squeak. "Don't let him bite me a third time—I could become *microscopic*—"

The Rat clutched Cheswick firmly around the middle and gave a violent twist. "It's your bad luck," he panted, "that my cage was once papered with *Wild & Woolly Wrestling*." He levered the little man to the floor, shifting his grip to a full nelson. "How does it feel to be *afraid*, Mr. Big Hand?"

"Wait. Don't scare him," said Brian, crossing the floor. "Come on, Uncle. I'll put you where you'll be safe."

"Put him in my cage," called Sissy cheerfully. "I won't be using it anymore."

The quivering lump that was Cheswick Vole looked up from Brian's hand, his eyes wide and terrified. "A . . . a *cage*? For *me*?"

"It's only for a little while," said Brian kindly. "I'll get water for your dish," he added, walking toward the back room, "and some fresh wood shavings . . ."

"But I just got *out* of jail!" The cry drifted plaintively over Brian's retreating shoulder until the velvet curtain cut it off. A minute later Brian returned, dusting his hands. "Okay, now what?"

The Rat cleared his throat. "No doubt you wish to thank me for gallant biting in the face of danger. But"—he held up a paw, smiling modestly—"I must hurry away; the lads are counting on me for pawball. I'm their most valuable player, you know."

Joe choked. Emmy turned away from the Rat as she struggled to keep a straight face.

The Rat addressed Brian with dignity. "Will you open the door, sir? Sissy, after you."

Emmy and Joe didn't laugh out loud until the door shut behind the rodents—and then they couldn't stop. Weak with reaction and relief, the professor's snores only made them laugh harder. At last, Brian picked them up in his calloused hand. "It's no laughing matter for Uncle Cheswick," he said sternly.

Emmy wiped her eyes, sobering. She didn't much like being picked up by a giant hand, and the thought reminded her of something else. "Crumbs—we forgot to have Sissy give us a kiss."

Joe shrugged. "We can always do that later. Besides, I'm not sure I want to grow yet. What am I going to say to my parents about where I was all this time?"

Emmy didn't answer. Her eye had wandered to the open cabinet. The left-hand side was fitted out with drawers and a narrow counter; the right side held shelves filled with small glass vials, each with its own label.

"I've never seen it unlocked before," Brian murmured, moving closer. He set Emmy and Joe on one of the shelves and peered in. "Essence of Hamster . . . Powdered Lemming Spoor . . . Distilled Prairie Dog Tail. What do all those do, I wonder?"

The inside of the cabinet smelled of wood and old varnish, with hints of more exotic smells lingering in the corners. Emmy walked around a bottle with a faded, peeling label. "Shrinking Rat Saliva—hey! This must be Raston's!"

"It's old, though," said Joe, tapping at the cloudy glass. "And it's almost all gone."

Brian nodded thoughtfully. "So some of the rodents' powers can be put in a bottle, I guess, and others you have to get directly from the rat itself."

"Like the chinchilla footprint," said Joe.

"But with Raston, it works both ways. He can bite you, or you can just swallow the spit from the bottle," Emmy pointed out. She eyed a vial whose contents had separated. The liquid went from deep purple at the base to bright yellow at the top, with small flakes of bright pink sediment suspended in the middle.

"Swallow Ratty's spit? Gross," said Joe, prowling among the bottles.

Brian shook his head. "Would you swallow it, or would you inject it with a needle? I mean, when Raston bites someone, his saliva goes straight into the bloodstream."

Emmy frowned. "True, but what about Sissy's kisses? They don't break the skin."

"Maybe her saliva is absorbed through the pores."

"Don't forget," Joe said, wiping grime from the label of a stained green bottle, "some of the rodent stuff has to be breathed in. Like when that Bushy-Tailed Rat sneezed in the professor's face and gave him the Snoozer virus."

Emmy paced the shelf, regretting her impatience with the professor. You could study this stuff for years and never figure it all out. And yet she *had* to figure something out, and fast, in order to stop Miss Barmy and somehow keep her parents in town.

"It's all so complicated," she said gloomily. "I wish there were some directions, somewhere." She reached the end of the shelf and turned around to resume her pacing. "I don't mean those research notes, either. I mean simple ones that you can really understand—hey! Look!"

Brian followed her gaze and swung the right cabinet door open even wider. There, on the inside of the door, was a chart. Though written in pencil, and faint and smudged in spots, it listed each rodent's name, along with a description of its effective power, how to use it, and the suggested dosage.

"Wow," said Joe.

"We hit the jackpot," said Emmy, beaming. "Want to lose weight? Look at this one: 'Trim-Bellied Squirrel. Makes the fat become thin. Pluck five belly hairs, snip fine, and steep in one cup hot celery juice until cool. Take two teaspoons daily for twenty-four days. Repeat as necessary.' "

"Sounds appetizing," said Joe. "What do you say we try one and see if the directions work?"

Emmy scanned the list for a clearly written entry. " 'Hairy Pawed Agouti. Grows thick hair fast.' "

Brian shifted his weight. "That one can't do any harm. He's in the back room, too."

"It's in the interest of science, anyway," said Joe as Brian returned with a long-legged, reddish gold rodent about the size of a cat. He set it on the desk and petted it gently as Emmy consulted the directions.

" 'Touch right forepaw to skin for thick, fast growing hair.' Where do you want the extra hair, Brian?"

Brian cradled the agouti in his arms. "I've always sort of wanted a beard," he said shyly, and stroked the agouti's paw over his chin.

A dense mat of light brown hair spread rapidly on Brian's face, making him look years older. He moved the paw to his upper lip, and a bushy mustache appeared in seconds.

"Cool!" He reached up to touch his new beard, entranced; but the agouti, grunting playfully, patted his nose with its paw. A sudden tuft of hair sprang from the tip and began to curl.

Brian nearly dropped the rodent in his alarm. "Oh *no*—" He ran to the back room, clanged the door to the agouti's cage, and dashed up the stairs to look in the mirror. A low moan could be heard through the floorboards.

Emmy tried to keep a straight face when Brian reappeared with scissors in his hand, snipping away at a long, lustrous beard and a particularly silky lock of nose hair. He went straight for the chart and ran his finger down the listings.

"Lasts two to three weeks," he read, dismayed. "If rash results, discontinue use and call a doctor."

"It could be worse," said Emmy. "It could be permanent."

Brian trimmed the tip of his nose again. "Hey, I think it's slowing down."

"With any luck, you'll only have to shave your nose a few times a day," said Joe, clinking amid the vials. "Listen, wasn't it Scent of Shrew that Cheswick was going to get for Miss Barmy? Here it is." He pointed to a dark red bottle, half-filled with liquid.

"'Scent of Shrew,'" Emmy read, straining her eyes to make out the tiny penciled words on the chart. "'To cause forgetfulness. Heat to diffuse scent; exposure time—'" She passed over a smudged phrase and skipped to the next line. "'Sensitized olfactory receptors induce selective forgetfulness when scent is re-encountered. Repeat every two weeks or as needed.'"

"So what does that mean in English?" Joe looked at Brian quizzically.

Brian's beard growth was definitely slowing. He clipped it short and tossed the hair in the wastebasket before studying the chart once more.

"Olfactory," he said slowly. "I studied that in science. That's one of the twelve cranial nerves."

"So it's in the brain," said Joe thoughtfully.

"It must be connected to your sense of smell, somehow," said Emmy.

Brian nodded. "It looks like there are two parts to using Scent of Shrew. First, you're supposed to heat it up so the scent is released into the air. After a while— I can't read how long—the smell is imprinted in the brain of anyone nearby."

"Could you heat it up with a candle?" Joe asked with sudden interest.

"Sure, I guess. If you smeared it on the top and sides of a candle, it would probably work."

Joe nudged Emmy. "We were right, then. It was in the candle, during silent reading—"

"While I was with that nutty Dr. Leander," said Emmy indignantly, "making up stuff for him to write down—"

"And everybody forgot you even existed, at least until it wore off."

"But why would people just forget about *me*, and nobody else?"

"That's the second part," said Brian. "All Miss Barmy had to do to make sure you were completely ignored was to put the same scent on you before you went to school. For two weeks or so, whenever anyone in class caught a whiff of it, they'd just sort of blank you out. Selective forgetfulness, see? Their eyes would see you, their ears would hear you, but their brains wouldn't register the fact."

Emmy narrowed her eyes. "So that explains why she was always dabbing something behind my ears, or rubbing weird gunk on my hands."

Brian nodded. "She could have put it in your shampoo, or made you drink it so it would be on your breath."

"It would be great stuff for a spy to use," Joe said with enthusiasm. "You'd be just as good as invisible, to the right people."

"It would wear off after a while, though," said Emmy, thinking back. "Kids would start to notice me, a little, and I'd think things were changing—and then all of a sudden, they'd look right through me again. I suppose that meant Miss Barmy had just made another classroom visit," she added grimly.

"She must have made sure she didn't smell it herself," said Brian suddenly. "I'll bet she plugged her nose with wax or something."

"Could be. She always sounded like she had a cold." Joe turned a narrow pink bottle and looked closely at the label. "Isn't this the other one the Barmster wanted?"

"Distilled Extract of Gerbil," Emmy read, squinting. "Maturity $\times$ 3. Full effects after 24 hours." The rest of the penciled entry was too faint to read, and she looked at Brian, bewildered. "What does that mean? If you use it, you become three times wiser or something?"

A small crease appeared between Brian's eyebrows. "Becoming more mature," he said slowly, "is a good thing. So why would Miss Barmy want something like that?"

Joe shrugged. "At least it can't hurt anybody."

There was a sudden, sharp rap at the door, as if someone had hit it with a stick.

Brian turned pale.

Inside the cabinet, Joe looked at Emmy in consternation. "That's her now."

Emmy's mouth went dry. "No—it can't possibly—"

"Yes it can," said Brian grimly. "Uncle Cheswick said she could come anytime, remember? And he promised her Scent of Shrew and—"

"Don't give it to her!" Emmy breathed.

"Of course not, but—" Brian straightened and looked over his shoulder. "Find me something I can give her instead," he said quickly as the door was rapped again, "and stay out of sight. I'll stall her while you look." He swung the cabinet doors nearly shut.

"Better cut your nose hair again," Emmy called.

"Right," muttered Brian, shooting a glance behind the cabinet. The professor had stopped snoring, but still looked sound asleep. Brian sighed and walked to the door, a pudgy teenager with a foot-long beard.

"Joe, what can we give her?" Emmy whispered, her heart pulsing like a bird's in her throat.

"I don't know!" Joe's whisper was almost as panicked as hers. "If only Ratty were here, he could shrink her like he did Cheswick—"

"That wouldn't work," said Emmy, feverishly searching the chart by the narrow crack of light Brian had left them. "Cheswick has been bitten before—Ratty told me—but Miss Barmy hasn't. She'd squish Ratty flat before he could bite her a second time." She took a series of deep breaths, as the professor had done, and felt herself calming down just a trifle—enough, at any rate, to think.

"Listen, Joe. You read the labels one by one. I'll check the chart."

Joe nodded vigorously, squinting at the nearest bottle. "Jerboa Juice," he said under his breath.

Emmy's eyes were becoming accustomed to the half light. "An infusion of courage," she read softly. "No good. We don't want her to become *braver*."

"All right, then—Springhare Spit."

"That one just makes people jumpy—keeps them awake."

She nearly jumped *herself* as Brian's voice sounded from the entryway, low and gruff. "Miss Barmy, I presume?"

"Where is Cheswick?" snapped Miss Barmy. "How many different assistants does he need?" Her cane rapped impatiently on the floor. "I have an emergency; he said he would have something ready for me."

"I'm very sorry, ma'am, but Unc—I mean, Mr. Vole—is busy."

"What do you mean, *busy*?"

The menace in Miss Barmy's voice turned Emmy's knees weak. She sat down abruptly on the shelf and gripped the edge with both hands.

"Ointment of Palm Squirrel," breathed Joe over her shoulder.

Emmy looked for the listing on the chart. "Removes fear of heights," it read; she shook her head. Was there *nothing* they could use to thwart Miss Barmy?

"I mean he can't . . . he's not able to see you,"
Brian floundered, waving his arms. Emmy watched
through the crack as his hand brushed against his
beard. His shoulders suddenly straightened, as if he
had found new confidence.

"To be honest," said Brian, smoothing his mustache, "he's behind bars."

"Not again!"

"He wasn't expecting it." Brian shook his head
sadly. "But he did say that you wanted . . . Scent of
Shrew, was it?"

"*And* Extract of Gerbil," she added as Brian went
to the cabinet. "Don't forget to put something in that
one to make it taste good."

"That settles it," whispered Joe, hauling the narrow pink bottle from the back row. "She wants it for
herself."

Emmy nodded. "If it was for me, she'd want it to
taste foul." She helped Joe push the bottle to the
front of the shelf.

Brian filled a little container from it and wrote
"Gerbil Extract × 3" on the label. He turned, almost
bumping into Miss Barmy.

"Please sit down, ma'am," he said nervously, trying to block Miss Barmy's view of the shelves. "I have to concentrate; I can't mix these with anyone looking over my shoulder."

"Oh, very well." The chair scraped, and hard fingernails began a steady tapping. "Make sure the Scent of Shrew is strong," Miss Barmy said petulantly. "The last batch wore off too soon."

"In that case," said Brian, turning his back to her, "I'll give you a little extra."

Emmy wordlessly pushed a dusty brown bottle at him. He glanced at the label, checked the chart, and grinned.

"Cheswick only gives me three drops each time." Miss Barmy sounded fretful.

"Then I'll give you ten," said Brian. He winked at Emmy as he measured out drops into a little container. "And if Mr. Vole complains, I shall tell him that you *asked* for it."

There was a little silence. Emmy thought she could almost hear Miss Barmy's eyelashes flutter as Brian approached her.

"Here's the Scent of Shrew. Now, when you use it, don't just drip it on. Smear it all over."

"On the candle?"

"That's right," said Brian. "Use your fingertips; their warmth will activate it even more strongly."

"Why didn't Cheswick ever tell me that?"

"He's not quite as experienced as I am," said Brian, stroking his beard.

The door closed behind Miss Barmy at last. Brian collapsed in a chair, slack with relief. And from behind the cabinet emerged a deep, rich chuckle.

"You've got a good head on your shoulders, boy," said Professor Capybara, lurching to his feet. "And a good deal of hair on your head, too!"

Brian grinned sheepishly. "I kind of like having a beard," he admitted, trimming the hair on his nose once more.

"I had a little trouble with the Hairy Pawed Agouti once, myself. It patted my elbow; I couldn't wear short sleeves for weeks. Now, what did I miss during my nap?"

"Cheswick came back, and Ratty shrank him," Joe said.

"He's in Cecilia's old cage for now," said Brian, "and you saw Miss Barmy come for her potions."

"I only woke up as she was leaving." The professor looked into the cabinet. "Did she ask for Scent of Shrew?"

"Yes, but we gave her Oil of Beaver instead," said Emmy. "The chart said it was guaranteed to sniff out a lie. It was the best we could do."

"At least it won't cause any problems, right?" Joe came forward to the edge of the shelf. "I mean, if the kids in the class smell it in the candle, and it helps them know when somebody's lying, that might even help them. At least they won't start to ignore Emmy again."

"I don't think it will affect the class," said Brian. "Oil of Beaver is absorbed through the skin. That's why I told her to smear it on with her fingers."

Emmy looked at him, alarmed. "Does that mean she's going to be able to tell when someone *else* is lying?"

The professor shook his head, smiling. "No, I believe it works the other way around. I can't recall exactly, and this chart is incomplete, of course, but I don't think it will make things worse." He chortled to himself, tilting his head back to read the fine print through his glasses. "On the contrary, I think you may have come up with the perfect thing for our Miss Barmy. Hee hee! Oh, yes indeed!"

"Don't get too happy, Professor," Emmy warned. "You don't need *another* nap. Besides, I still need to grow and get home."

"You're right, my dear," said Professor Capybara, wiping his eyes. "I'll endeavor to remain calm. But I think what you gave her will work quite well; we'll find out tomorrow."

"So now," said Emmy, "we just have to pick something that will work for my parents. See, the chinchilla footprint has been wearing off, but it takes longer and longer each time."

Professor Capybara looked suddenly serious.

"But if we can just get them to stay in town, maybe we can figure out an antidote, or something."

The professor nodded. "All right, my dear. I have my notes here, and the bottles in the cabinet, and the rodents in the back room. I'll do my best to help." He looked around the floor. "But where have Cecilia and Raston gone?"

"Pawball," said Emmy and Joe together.

"Bring them back here, would you please? You need Sissy's kiss to grow—and in the meantime, perhaps

I can find something for you. Now, Brian, where does Cheswick keep my charascope?"

The game was still in its second quarter; there had been a lot of time-outs. "Every time a cat comes by," Mrs. Bunjee explained, "or anyone else at all, the lookouts whistle and we all dive for the nearest gopher hole. Once, that awful Mrs. Bee across the street woke up and threw a flowerpot, and we all stayed underground until her light went out."

Joe turned his head. "Threw a flowerpot? She must be nuts."

"But isn't Raston playing? And where's Sissy?" Emmy scanned the field, but it was hard to pick one rodent out from the mass of furry backs jostling in the moonlight for a small, leather ball.

"I haven't been paying much attention, dear—I've been collecting dew and seeds for halftime. This red wagon of yours is lovely for snacks!"

Emmy didn't answer, for she had just located the Rat. He was on the sidelines, his shoulders hunched, and he was not wearing a jersey.

Joe shoved his hands in his pockets. "Do you see Sissy anywhere?"

Emmy shook her head.

"I'll scout around," said Joe, drifting off through the scrubby grass.

A whistle blew, sharp and shrill. Buck's voice rose clearly from the field. "Okay, Chippy, Traft's hurt. Who do we have for a sub?"

The Rat cleared his throat loudly. Chippy ignored him.

"Scurrie, you go in for Traft," said Chippy in a low voice to a ground squirrel.

"But what about *meeee?*" Emmy heard the Rat wail as the whistle blew again.

"Listen, Ratso, or whatever your name is," said Chippy, his voice rising in exasperation, "I've told you and told you. You're not on the team! You haven't practiced with us—I don't know if you're any good—"

Mrs. Bunjee's head went up. "Nonsense, Chipster. Of course Raston can play if he wants to. He's our *guest.*" She marched to the pile of jerseys, ignoring Chippy's look of anguish. "What's your size, Raston?"

"*S,* for speedy," said the Rat, swaggering a little.

"*Fweeet! Fweeeeet!*" The whistle blew twice, louder and more piercing than before. The rodents poured off the field and mobbed the snack cart. The Rat smoothed his jersey with a fond paw and explained the fine points of the game to anyone who would listen.

"*Fweeet!*" went the whistle again, and both teams trotted to the center line. Raston, swinging his paws with athletic enthusiasm, trotted to the halfback position and got down on all fours.

"He's going to get creamed," said Emmy gloomily.

18

EMMY SAT HUDDLED on a little rise of grass, watching the progress of the game. She knew she should help Joe search for Cecilia, but she couldn't quite make herself do it. It had to be three in the morning, or even later, and her brain felt fuzzy.

"*Fweeet!*" The whistle blew again. The referee shook his paw at Raston and held up a yellow card. "Tail pulling. Penalty kick."

Emmy watched as one of the gophers took three long steps and kicked the ball up past a line of defenders. It sliced just inside a corner of the twig-and-grass goal, and the gophers erupted into wild cheering.

Emmy sighed. Miss Barmy must be home by now. In another half hour—or forty-five minutes, at the most—she would be sound asleep, and Emmy could go home and to bed.

"I found Sissy," said Joe, leading her by the paw. He glanced over his shoulder at the game. "What's the score?"

"I was looking at the stars," Cecilia said happily. "I hope I didn't worry you, but I haven't seen them for so long, and I couldn't understand pawball anyway—"

"*He's got the ball!*" Joe shouted. "Ratty's got the ball!"

The Rat, shrieking with joy, raced down the field, his plump body jiggling, his tail held straight out behind him, maneuvering the hard leather ball between his feet. The gophers seemed to be giving him no opposition; instead, they were watching him with open mouths.

"Oh my goodness," cried Cecilia delightedly, "Raston has totally confused the other team!"

"They're confused, all right," said Joe, "because he's going the—"

"WRONG WAY!" screamed Chippy, outraged. "TURN *AROUND,* YOU STUPID RAT!"

But it was too late. The Rat, happy, oblivious, grunting with fierce determination, dodged past his own shocked goalie and kicked the ball squarely in the net.

"*Nooooo!*" howled Chippy. Raston, panting and triumphant, turned around with a modest smile—and was immediately mobbed by his furious teammates. The gophers howled with laughter, holding their tiny stomachs.

"Oh, dear," said Cecilia.

Chippy, grinding his teeth, stalked onto the field. Buck spoke earnestly with the referee.

"Get off the field!" yelled a ground squirrel, yanking at the Rat's white jersey.

"But I get to play!" Raston protested. "Chippy *said*!"

"That was before you played like a *hamster*, you moron! You absolutely destroyed our lead!"

"But we can get it back," cried the Rat eagerly. "Just give me the ball—"

He squealed in panic as a guinea pig and a gray squirrel grabbed him by the paws and began to swing him back and forth. Their teammates cheered, clapping wildly.

"We're going to forfeit the game," cried Joe, sprinting onto the field.

The moon, just sinking behind the tops of trees, laid long shadows on the pawball field and brushed the edge of the surging crowd of rodents with light.

And for one brief instant, it shone mercilessly on the Rat as he soared above the heads of his teammates, his limbs flailing and his mouth open in a long, drawn-out "EEEEEEEEEeeeee!"

There was a thump and an agonized cry as he landed in the net and took it down with him, twigs and all.

"Ow, ow ow owie! IT HURTS, YOU'VE BROKEN MY ANKLE, YOU *BARBARIANS*—"

"*Fweeeeeeeet!*" The referee blew his whistle and glared wrathfully. "That's a red card to the guinea pig. You're out of the game. Red card to the gray squirrel, out of the game—no, sir, you may *not* substitute when a player has been red carded."

Emmy grabbed the wagon and rattled onto the field. By the time she reached the Rat, Buck had pulled him out of the goal and laid him, whimpering, on the grass.

"Okay, calm down." Buck took hold of the Rat's ankle. "Can you bend it like this? How about like this?"

"Ow ow ow owie ow ow IT HURTS—"

"Shut up," Buck said briefly, dusting off his knees. "Okay, it's just a sprain. Ice it and wrap it up, and he'll be okay. But he won't be playing pawball any-time soon."

He turned to Chippy. "Who should we sub for him?"

Chippy looked worried. "I don't know," he mut-tered. "With two players red carded, it's probably hopeless anyway."

Joe stepped forward. "I'll go in, if you want." He glanced from Chippy to Buck. "I play soccer all the time at school. I'm not too bad."

Buck looked at him thoughtfully. "Last week I climbed the schoolyard oak and watched some kid with yellow hair make goal after goal. By any chance, was that—"

"It was me," said Joe. "So, can I play?"

"There you are," said Emmy. "All tucked in." She looked fondly at the Rat, who was wedged into the dolls' wagon, his feet hanging out and his nose pointed skyward. "Are you ready to go?"

The Rat wiped his eyes with a listless paw. "What does it matter?" he said, sniffling. "I'm a d—di—disgrace, that's what they all think—"

"Well," said Emmy, "not *all* of them."

"They *laughed* at me," said the Rat. "No one mentioned how well I dribbled the ball! Or how clever I was to get it past the goalie!"

"That's true," said Emmy, pulling the wagon toward the sidelines. "*I* noticed, though."

"My ankle could get worse," said the Rat darkly. "I might die. And then they'll be sorry."

"They're sorry now," said Emmy.

"Not sorry enough," said the Rat, and his eyes filled with tears.

As Sissy and Mrs. Bunjee joined them, Emmy glanced at the field where the pawball game had gotten under way once more. Joe, his thatch of hair white in the starlight, was seemingly everywhere at once—dribbling, passing, shouting for the ball. As she watched, he headed a corner kick into the far goal, and cheering came faintly to her ears, high and shrill.

They headed over to the Antique Rat to find a bandage.

"How's that?" asked Brian, kneeling on the floor as Mrs. Bunjee tied a final knot in the handkerchief around the Rat's ankle. "Better?"

"I . . . can bear it," said the Rat, flinging an arm over his eyes.

"Brave Rasty!" said Sissy, patting his paw.

"But the physical agony," he sniffled, "is nothing compared with my blighted hopes. I had such dreams of being a star."

"But Raston," said Mrs. Bunjee persuasively, "you can be a star at something *else*."

The Rat looked doubtful. "Like what?"

"Er—" said Mrs. Bunjee. "I'm sure there are *lots* of special things you can do. You can bite . . . and *shrink* people, and . . . and . . ." She looked at Emmy and Sissy for inspiration.

"I can sing 'The Star-Spangled Banner,'" the Rat said suddenly.

"Well, there you go! Not every rat can do *that*!"

The Rat wiped his nose with his sleeve and sat up. "Would you like to hear me?"

"Sometime I shall *love* to hear you," said Mrs. Bunjee, patting his knee. "But right now you need to rest."

"And I need to grow," said Emmy, presenting her cheek to Sissy to be kissed.

She had been expecting it, but still she felt as if she had been launched from a cannon, straight up. Emmy looked down at the rodents, suddenly small, and wandered over to the desk where Professor Capybara was bent above an odd-looking microscope.

It was made of pewter and polished brass and had two eyepieces, several small jointed arms, and a multitude of knobs. Emmy pulled up a chair. "What are you looking at?"

"Greed, hope, fear, and joy," said the professor, beaming. "Here, have a look."

Emmy slid over to look through the eyepiece. Small, glowing shapes swam before her eyes, lit from beneath and vividly colored. As she watched, two shapes joined, flipped over, and duplicated themselves, creating in a moment a whole new shape.

"What kind of microscope is this?" Emmy asked, unable to take her eyes off the swimming life beneath.

"It's not a microscope—it's a charascope. My own invention, and the only one in the world. If you've ever wondered about the building blocks of

character, well"—the professor chuckled joyfully—
"there they are."

"But how can you tell what you're looking at?"

"You get a certain feeling when you look long
enough," said the professor vaguely. "But of course
I applied scientific methods. Trial and error, my
dear, and long study. I was doing clinical trials before
Cheswick shrank me, and they looked very promising
indeed. What you see now are the character elements
found in just one drop of my own blood."

Emmy blinked as a long, twisted, dark green
shape came writhing across her field of vision.
"What's that worm-looking thing?"

The professor gave it one quick glance and looked
away. "Ah, yes . . . I thought that would show up,
sooner or later."

"But what *is* it?"

"You could call it resentment, I suppose. Anger
and fear mixed. I really am quite angry at Cheswick
Vole for what he did to me, you see, and that
worm will infect my whole system unless I attend
to it."

Emmy looked at him attentively. "What would
happen if you didn't take care of it?"

"Oh, it would keep growing, adding bits, connecting with other unpleasant shapes floating around. I imagine in the end it could become something quite monstrous."

"Are you going to mix up some kind of rodent potion to get rid of it?"

The professor sighed. "If only it were that easy. No, there's only one way to dissolve that particular worm, I'm afraid. But still," the professor went on, "rodent powers often do affect character, as you have so cleverly guessed. The chinchilla, which Miss Barmy used to such striking effect on your parents, is a case in point."

"What I'd like to know," said Emmy, "is how the chinchilla print works. How can one single pawprint make my parents stop caring about me? And why is it taking longer and longer to wear off?"

The professor leaned back in his chair and rubbed his eyes. "The chinchilla's particular gift," he said, "is to switch things around. To make what was once important, unimportant, and vice versa. It was mostly used on adolescent members of tribal societies who were slow to take on the responsibilities of adulthood. For example, a lazy young man who preferred playing his flutelo to working would, after eating a meal trodden upon by the chinchilla, suddenly begin to catch fish and mend nets. Interestingly enough," the professor added thoughtfully, "he would also stop slouching—"

"But my parents already *were* responsible!" Emmy interrupted.

"Exactly. You had been important to them, so when they ate the cookies that had the chinchilla's footprint, all that they felt was important, including you, suddenly seemed of little value. Now, how had your parents felt about other things before meeting Miss Barmy? How had they felt about impressing people, for example? Were they, by any chance, very polite to people who were important in some way, and rude to those they considered beneath them?"

"Never!" said Emmy heatedly. "They were nice to everyone. There was this old raggedy man who came in our bookstore sometimes, and my father told me once that you could never tell about people—because that old man, who looked like a bum off the street, only read the very best kind of books."

She paused, remembering. "My father would let old Bill sit and just read for hours, and lots of times he couldn't afford to buy anything. But my dad didn't care. He'd pour him a cup of coffee, and my mom would bring a plate of cookies, and they'd all sit and talk about books. "

The professor smiled. "Your parents sound like people I'd like to meet."

Emmy looked away. "You wouldn't like them now. They're only interested in clothes, and snobby parties, and salmon fishing in Alaska."

"*Exactly!*" said the professor. "Your parents have had their values, their true values, turned upside down. Why do you think the footprint keeps wearing off?"

Emmy shrugged. "Because it doesn't last?"

"But it's *meant* to last!" The professor sat up straight. "Don't you see? In the tribes, usually one or two meals imprinted by a chinchilla were enough to bring the lazy person back to the values he'd been taught. But with your parents, what the chinchilla does to them is so *diametrically* opposed to their true values—so *completely* at odds with what they really believe—"

"—that their true feelings keep struggling to come out!" Emmy clapped her hands.

"Precisely. They must love you a great deal, my dear. But you say that it is taking longer and longer for them to recover now?"

Emmy nodded. "Last summer they'd only go away for the weekend. It got to be more in the fall. Then they almost missed Christmas—and the last trip they took lasted five weeks and four days."

The professor looked very serious. "I am very much afraid, my dear, that your parents can't hold out against the chinchilla's effect forever. One of these days Miss Barmy may turn their values around for good."

Emmy shoved back her chair. "How do I know it hasn't happened already?" She gripped the chair arms and steadied her voice. "I know you've been trying to find something to bring them back to normal. *Please* give me whatever you've found; I can use it tonight."

The professor's neck flushed. "Emmy, I'm so very sorry, but I got sidetracked with the charascope, you see. I was just going to have one look, but . . . well . . . it's terribly fascinating . . ."

Emmy swallowed the reproachful words that rose in her throat. As the professor ran his hands through his hair, looking distraught and embarrassed, she took hold of his arm. "It's okay, Professor. Just stay calm, all right?"

Professor Capybara shut his eyes. He breathed deeply some twenty times, and the red flush faded. "I haven't found it yet," he said at last. "But I'm sure there will be *something* you can use."

Emmy let go of his arm abruptly. "Wait a second—how about the Endear Mouse! It makes the absent heart grow fonder, the tag says. And it wants to help me, I know it does."

Professor Capybara was grave as he walked to the back room. "Is that right?" he asked the Endear Mouse. "Do you want to go with Emmy, to try to counteract the effects of the chinchilla?"

The little mouse nodded.

"Even knowing what that means for you?" The professor spoke very gently.

"What? What does it mean?" asked Emmy, glancing from the professor to the mouse.

The Endear Mouse nodded again, looking determined.

"Very well," said the professor, hanging a small tag around its neck. "Here are the directions, Emmy. Don't read them until you get to your room."

Brian and Emmy stood in the shadows near her back door, listening. No sound came from the house; no light shone through the windows.

They had picked up her backpack on the way. Raston and Cecilia had hung out of the side pockets, while the Endear Mouse had preferred to ride on her shoulder.

"Do you have your key?" Brian whispered.

Emmy nodded. "Good night," she whispered as she slipped inside.

"Mrrrrow?"

The rodents squeaked. Muffy strolled into the kitchen as coolly as if she had spent the night on her own kitty bed, rather than terrorizing innocent little creatures.

"I know what you did last night," Emmy whispered, looking sternly into the yellow green eyes shining in the darkened kitchen. "Bad Muffy. *Bad*."

Muffy stared back, looking bored, and padded silently up the stairs to the housekeeper's room. Emmy followed, strongly tempted to indulge in a little cat kicking; the Endear Mouse was trembling on her shoulder.

Once safely in her bedroom, Emmy took the rodents to the dollhouse. Raston and Sissy seemed glad to curl up on the beds, but the Endear Mouse wouldn't let go.

"All right," said Emmy, walking back to her bed. "You can sleep on my pillow, if you want."

The Endear Mouse ran down Emmy's sleeve and jumped onto the bed. Then it turned and hugged her bare wrist, its arms as far around as they could reach.

"Bad cat," said a small voice.

Emmy looked at the mouse, startled. "Did you speak?"

The Endear Mouse looked confused. It withdrew its paw and shook its head.

"But I heard you say, 'Bad cat.' I didn't know you could speak."

The mouse edged closer and touched Emmy's hand again. "I can't."

Emmy stared at the tiny face. The mouth hadn't opened. Yet she had heard the words as plain as anything.

"Can you . . . hear me?" The eyes of the Endear Mouse widened in question as the words made their way into Emmy's mind.

"Yes!" whispered Emmy. "When you touch me—I can hear you think!"

The Endear Mouse's face lit with joy, and Emmy laughed, delighted. The mouse had touched her before, but always so briefly that Emmy hadn't registered its thoughts. And now—what an amazing thing!

The mouse bounced on Emmy's pillow, kicking its legs and laughing. Then it curled itself up in a little ball of fluff, tucked its nose beneath its paws, and nestled down to sleep.

The instruction tag was still around its neck, and looked uncomfortable. Emmy found small scissors in her bedside table and carefully cut the string. The tag came free and opened in her hand. Taped to the inside was a needle, long and sharp and hollow.

"'Endear Mouse,'" she read. "'Makes the absent heart grow fonder. Steep one hair from the beloved in three drops of heart's blood. Survival of the mouse is *not* guaranteed.'"

19

EMMY STIRRED, opened her eyes, and gazed for a moment at the sun on her pillow. It lay golden across her hand and the sleeping Endear Mouse, shining through the window blinds in stripes of shadow and light.

Emmy's eye was inches from the mouse. She could see the small pink nose, and the closed eyes, and the gossamer fur that rose and fell with each quick breath. Carefully, delicately, Emmy moved her hand, just touching the mouse's tiny chest.

The pulse was rapid, as rapid as a bird's. She could feel it beating against her fingertip.

What, exactly, was she supposed to do with the hollow needle? Plunge it into the mouse's little heart? And *then* what?

Emmy shut her eyes. She imagined herself putting the drops of blood on her parents' hairs, while the Endear Mouse lay dying—

She opened her eyes abruptly, willing away the thought. Her gaze fell on the little frame on her bedside table, and her parents' smiling faces.

No. The tag didn't say the mouse would die. It just said "Survival of the mouse is not *guaranteed.*" Most times, it would probably live.

On the other hand, she wasn't just talking about making one heart grow fonder. She was talking about *two.* That would mean two hairs—one from each of her parents. That would mean *six* drops of blood.

Emmy looked at the mouse, small and defenseless.

And then she made a decision.

She would not do it.

Emmy sat up and threw back the covers. She wasn't going to think about this anymore. She had decided. Even if her parents went away again, even if it took *months* for the chinchilla effect to wear off, even if she was stuck with Miss Barmy all that time, she would not use the Endear Mouse, and everything would still turn out fine in the end. Because this time she had Joe and the professor and Raston and Brian to help her, not to mention Mrs. Bunjee and Buck and Chippy and Sissy and all the rest.

Emmy leaped out of bed and brushed her hair vigorously. *That* was why Miss Barmy had gone to the school and done her weird atmostherapy, trying to make sure that no one ever noticed her. Friends are people who help when things go wrong; but Miss Barmy had wanted her to be alone, without any help at all.

"Well, I've got friends *now*," said Emmy, throwing down her brush and opening the window.

"I want to look out, too," said the Rat from the playroom door. "Fresh air is good for sprained ankles, right?"

"Probably," said Emmy, lifting the Rat to the windowsill. "Good morning, Ratty."

"Afternoon, I'd say." He leaned out and tried to grab a fluttering oak leaf.

Emmy looked at the clock, startled. It was past lunchtime! Of course she had been up most of the night, so it wasn't surprising that she had slept so long. But why hadn't anyone gotten her up for school?

There was a brisk knock. Maggie bumped the door open with her hip and came in carrying a glass on a tray.

"So you're finally awake, Em—EEEEEEEK!"

"Shhh—don't scream, *please*—"

"It's a RAT!" Maggie's whisper sounded like a tiny screech.

"It's . . . it's dead," said Emmy quickly, turning the Rat over on his back. He grinned sardonically, let his eyes roll back in his head, and kept his paws stiff in the air. Even in her panic, Emmy had to admire his acting talent. He looked as if he had been dead for days.

"What on earth," Maggie said hoarsely, "are you doing with a dead rat?"

"It's a science project," Emmy said, glancing at her pillow in time to see the Endear Mouse scurry off the bed. "Please don't tell Miss Barmy, *please.*"

Maggie looked at her doubtfully. "But a *rat*—"

"Please please please please please *please*—"

Maggie sighed. "Oh, all right. But keep it out of sight, and if it starts to smell—"

"I'll get rid of it," Emmy promised. "Um, why didn't anyone wake me up for school?"

"Miss Barmy wanted you to stay home today," Maggie said, plumping Emmy's pillow and pulling up the covers.

"Why?" Emmy asked, but immediately knew the answer. Miss Barmy had planned to do "atmostherapy" today. Of course she didn't want Emmy around.

"She says your nutritional balance is upset—"

Emmy rolled her eyes.

"—and she says you have to drink this—"

Emmy looked at the glass filled with blue liquid and shuddered.

"—and then rest all day because your parents want you at their charity event tonight—"

"Really?"

"—for exactly two minutes, to be shown off."

"Oh." Emmy hesitated. "Maggie, why tonight? My parents usually don't want me around when they have a party."

She waited for the answer, holding her breath. Was the chinchilla footprint wearing off early for some reason?

Maggie opened the door to the hall. "It's because the event is for the Society for the Protection of Abandoned and Neglected Kids. The chairman thought it would be nice to have a real child there, and you happen to be around."

"Oh," said Emmy, as Maggie closed the door gently behind her.

There was a derisive snort from the Rat as he sat up, massaging his arms. "She has *got* to be kidding. 'The Society for the Protection of Abandoned and Neglected Kids'?"

"S.P.A.N.K.," said Cecilia brightly, emerging from the toyroom.

"Why don't they protect *you*?" Raston demanded, skidding into the room, his ankle apparently all better. "Why don't they stay at home for once, and get rid of that loathsome nanny, and stop neglecting their own daughter?"

Emmy had no answer. She poured the glass of blue liquid into the toilet and flushed.

"Come on, Sissy," said the Rat, taking his sister's paw. "You, too, Endear. I want to show you the train. It really goes!"

Emmy, hungry after missing both breakfast and lunch, headed for the kitchen. She was halfway down the grand staircase when she heard Miss Barmy's voice below.

"I have enough on my mind without your interference."

Emmy stopped dead on the stairs and turned to face the wall. It was covered with old portraits. They had come with the house and no one had ever bothered to take them down, and they were as good an excuse as any for standing motionless on the steps. She gazed at a picture of an old man in a pinstriped suit who looked familiar.

Well, of course he looked familiar . . . she must have walked by his portrait a thousand times. Emmy stared blankly at his gold tie pin and listened carefully.

"I *know* the charity event is tonight, Mrs. Brecksniff, but I absolutely *had* to visit Emmaline's school today—uoough—"

Miss Barmy's voice stopped suddenly with a little grunt, and all at once the entryway echoed with a rich, ripe, startlingly loud fart.

There was a stunned silence below. Emmy peeked over the banister. And then the odor hit her, rolling toward her nose with the power of an exploding bomb. It was, quite simply, the worst thing she had ever smelled. A combination of old garbage and decaying flesh and skunk all together might possibly be as bad, but she doubted it.

"Perhaps some fresh air," said Maggie hastily, opening a window.

"I meant to say," Miss Barmy amended quickly, "that it was important to *me* to visit Emmaline's school today."

The smell disappeared at once. Miss Barmy, who had faltered for a moment, soldiered on. "The florist is arriving at four, the caterers at five, and the bartenders at six, but I shall be attending to Emmaline." She paused, experimentally. There was no smell.

"She is my *first* priority, you understand," Miss Barmy added, and promptly let loose another ear-splitter.

Mrs. Brecksniff gagged audibly. There was a low moan from Maggie. Emmy plugged her nose a second too late.

Miss Barmy raised her voice angrily. "Well, maybe not my *very* first priority, but her nutritional balance is at a critical point, she *needs* me to watch over her— *aiiiieeee!*" She let another one rip, even worse than before.

Mrs. Brecksniff fanned the air desperately with both hands. Maggie put her head right out the window and gasped for air.

"I'm only concerned for her well-being!" shrieked Miss Barmy and ran up the stairs without even seeing Emmy, followed by a rapid-fire burst of popping gas and a cloud of noxious fumes.

The horrible smell lingered a moment, then was abruptly gone. Mrs. Brecksniff and Maggie stared up in wonder.

"That," murmured Mrs. Brecksniff, awestruck, "was enough to choke a *buffalo*."

"Did you notice," said Maggie slowly, "it only seemed to happen when she said something that— well, that was probably—"

"A *lie*," whispered Emmy, realization dawning. A wide grin spread over her face as she remembered the dusty brown bottle she and Joe had pushed across the shelf to Brian. Oil of Beaver—guaranteed to sniff out a lie! And Brian had told Miss Barmy to be sure to smear it on with her fingertips . . .

Emmy ran back upstairs and stopped outside Miss Barmy's door. The nanny's voice was high with hysteria.

"And not only didn't it work at school, but now every time I say anything to anybody, there's this awful *smell*—"

Emmy could hear Miss Barmy pacing back and forth.

"I don't care what the label said, it didn't work!" Miss Barmy shrilled. "I smeared it on the candle like you said, and then the very *minute* I was finished, that teacher—Heesabore, whatever his name is—asked about Emmaline! He *remembered* her! Oh, it was terrible. I had no influence over them at all!"

Emmy walked to her father's office and picked up the phone very quietly, muffling the mouthpiece with her hand.

"My dear Miss Barmy, I see it now," said Professor Capybara's soothing voice over the wire. "Scent of Shrew was on the shelf right next to Oil of Beaver. My assistant must have gotten the two confused."

"Your *assistant*? Who are you, then?"

"I am Professor Capybara, Cheswick Vole's new partner. While Cheswick is . . . unavailable, I take full responsibility for any problems that may arise."

"Well, you can start by firing that fool with the long beard and hairy nose!"

"My dear lady," said Professor Capybara's reassuring voice, "I know this must be terribly upsetting. But the oil should wear off in a few days—"

"A FEW DAYS?" shouted Miss Barmy. Emmy held the receiver slightly away from her ear.

"—but until then, I strongly suggest that you tell the truth. The Oil of Beaver, absorbed through the skin, allows everyone in your vicinity to sniff out a lie, so to speak. As long as you tell the truth you'll have no problem."

"STOP *LYING*? ARE YOU *SERIOUS*?"

"Madam, you are the customer," said the professor. "Tell me what you require. I shall do everything in my power to assist you."

"Everything is going *wrong*! I'm losing *control*! And there's a big party tonight, and the Addisons have to be carefully watched—my plans are almost in place, but I can't even leave my room, this terrible smell sends everyone absolutely *running* from me—"

"My dear lady, calm yourself. I have the solution. I shall attend the party and monitor the Addisons myself, and give you immediate warning should they show any signs of—well—whatever it is you don't want."

"It's an exclusive party. They won't let you in."

The professor chuckled. "Ever since I invented the Universal Rodent Translator, I have been in demand as a party guest; my years out of circulation will only have added to my mystery. I should be very surprised if I weren't welcomed with open arms."

"But there's the brat to deal with still," Miss Barmy wailed.

"The—brat?"

"Emmaline. She's getting worse and worse, I kept her in her room all day today but I won't be able to watch her tonight. This disgusting smell follows me *everywhere*—"

"Ah." Professor Capybara coughed slightly. "If you will allow me to act as her attendant this evening, I can make sure she is adequately supervised. I know a fair amount of child psychology."

"That doesn't work on her, I've *tried*—"

"Well, then, would you like me to use more traditional techniques? Arm twisting, nose tweaking, hair yanking—"

"Yes! Yes!"

"—along with bullying, pretended concern, and shame—"

"We understand each other perfectly," said Miss Barmy. "And just to make absolutely sure that she's under control, I want you to bring the chinchilla. Stamp its paw into something that children like to eat, and make sure Emmaline eats it. In fact, I want to see her eat it myself."

"But my dear Miss Barmy," began the professor, "what good will that do?"

"She won't drop any more cats on my potato rolls, for one thing," snapped Miss Barmy, and she hung up with a bang.

There was silence on the other end, and then a deep sigh.

Emmy hastily removed her hand from the mouthpiece. "Professor Capybara?" she whispered. "It's me, Emmy. Listen—I have an idea."

20

Emmy skipped down the hall and skidded into her room with a pleased sense that things were going very well, indeed.

"Oh, saaay can you seeee, by the daaawnzer lee liiight . . ."

Emmy approached the playroom door on tiptoe. Someone was singing in a rather husky baritone. She poked her head cautiously around the corner. The Rat was on the stage of the puppet theater, looking self-conscious.

"Lovely!" said Mrs. Bungee, clapping her paws. "I *knew* you had a special talent, Raston!"

"But I'm not a *star*," said the Rat glumly.

"You just need an audience," said Mrs. Bungee. She chittered loudly, and all over the playroom, rodent heads popped up.

"Come, everyone!"

Chippy left the train with a clatter of tools. The Endear Mouse and Sissy came at a run from the art center, their paws red with fingerpaint. And Buck, who had been trying out Emmy's peashooter, bounced across the room with Joe clinging to a harness on his back. Emmy, watching with interest, wondered if they had traveled like that all the way from Rodent City— but Mrs. Bunjee was asking for quiet.

Mrs. Bunjee smiled encouragingly at the Rat. "Now, Raston, you have your audience."

"No—I don't really think—," said the Rat, twisting his paws.

"Come now, Raston," Mrs. Bunjee said bracingly. "Sing! Sing from your heart!"

The Rat cleared his throat, opened his mouth— and shut it again. He looked at them helplessly. There was an uncomfortable pause.

"He's scared," said Chippy, snickering.

"Stage fright," Buck said, getting up as if to go. "It happens sometimes."

Sissy's nose turned a deeper shade of pink. "My brother is *not* afraid. He's just—" She looked at Raston appealingly.

"I'm just saving my voice," said the Rat faintly, looking at Sissy.

"Saving it? For what?" Chippy sounded skeptical.

"For—for—"

"Careful, Ratty," warned Emmy.

"For the party tonight," the Rat went on recklessly. "I was asked to sing at the fund-raiser for the Society for the Protection of Abandoned and Neglected Kids."

Sissy clapped her paws in delight.

"Here we go," murmured Joe.

"Oh, really? What are you going to sing?" Chippy challenged.

The Rat stiffened. "An . . . original song," he stammered.

No one had a response to this.

"I'd invite you all," said the Rat hurriedly, "but it wouldn't be safe. No dark corners to hide in, you know."

Chippy's face broke into a slow grin. "I'll bet I could find one. I wouldn't miss this for the *world*."

Mrs. Bunjee cut in. "Tell me, Raston. This song—have you finished writing it?"

The Rat cleared his throat. "Not . . . not quite."

"Well, then," Mrs. Bunjee said with decision, "we must leave you alone to write. We will find that dark corner now, before all the people come, and wait there to hear your *beautiful* song."

"Hey, Buck, what about the air ducts?" suggested Chippy. "Couldn't we crawl straight through to the room where he's going to—uh—sing?"

"Sure, we could do that." Buck scratched his head and looked around. "There's a ball of kite string, and we can let it out to find our way back. Emmy, would you open that vent in the wall?"

Emmy averted her eyes from the Rat's worried little face and pulled off the vent cover so the rodents could climb inside. She gave the Endear Mouse a boost up, then waved good-bye.

"Look for the room with the piano," she called down the heat duct, and the scrabbling sound of tiny claws gradually faded away.

The Rat buried his head in his paws.

Joe, who had lagged behind, shook his head. "Too bad, Ratty, but you asked for it."

"Oh, shut up," the Rat snapped. "Why don't you do something useful and get me a pencil and paper?"

Emmy's idea required clay. She had begun to mold a piece between her palms, and Joe was heading for the air vent, when she remembered something.

253

"How did the pawball game go?" she whispered, glancing at the Rat who was scribbling furiously in the corner.

Joe grinned. "We won after all. I got voted Most Valuable Rodent."

Emmy tried not to laugh. "Without a tail?"

Joe climbed into the open air duct. "No joke, Emmy, I had the greatest time. I *love* that game. I'm playing again tonight, and they actually made me a starter."

"But I thought you were sick of playing soccer?" Emmy pulled and pressed her small sculpture, frowning in concentration. She had to get this right.

"I'm sick of being *forced* to play," Joe said moodily. "And being screamed at from the sidelines. And having to practice all the time. Sometimes I wish I was like my little brother—pudgy and no talent at all."

He gazed down into the dark tunnel and took hold of the kite string that led into its depths.

"I have to do it all year—fall soccer, indoor soccer, traveling team, soccer camp." He shrugged. "I suppose I should have let Sissy grow me by now, but I *like* being small. It gives me time to be a kid."

Emmy watched as Joe disappeared into the metal duct. She knew what he meant. She had been signed up for ballet and gymnastics and French, basket weaving and gardening and little theater and—she couldn't even remember what else. Why did everything have to be so organized?

She gazed at the clay object she had made, satisfied, and let herself out of the room without bothering the Rat, who was chewing on his pencil with an air of concentration. She was really hungry now. She'd get something to eat, and bake the sculpture in the oven at the same time to harden it.

Emmy headed down to the kitchen. She paused halfway down the grand staircase to avoid a collision with the florists, who were filling the house with masses of flowers and what seemed to be a forest of potted palms.

"—and that's the reception room through there."  Mrs. Brecksniff, bustling as usual, passed through the foyer below, giving directions to three people at once. "We need flowers in the entryway, the hall, and in every bathroom. You can set up the bar over in that corner and let Maggie know if you need anything."

Emmy, waiting on the stairs, looked again at the portrait of the old gentleman in the pinstriped suit. He *did* look familiar . . .

"Mrs. Brecksniff?"

"Eh?" The housekeeper looked up, her face red and hot. "You're supposed to stay in bed, according to—" She stopped, and her face grew darker. "Well, you don't look sick to me," she finished, with her hands on her hips.

"I'm not." Emmy looked down at her calmly. "I don't know why she wants me to stay in my room, but I feel fine."

"She has her own reasons, no doubt," said Mrs. Brecksniff explosively, "but they make no sense to me, and I don't intend to worry about it anymore, and that's flat!"

Emmy nodded. It was the same sort of feeling she'd had when she first opened the Rat's schoolroom cage. She had felt it, too, when she had turned down the dark and dangerous alley—and again when she had sneaked out of the house at midnight. It was the feeling that she wasn't going to let Miss Barmy control her anymore. That she, Emmy, had something to say about her own life.

"Mrs. Brecksniff," Emmy said again, turning back to the portrait. "Who is this man? Do you know?"

Mrs. Brecksniff trod heavily up the stairs, breathing hard, and stopped just below Emmy. "Why," she said, "that's old William Addison. He was your father's great-uncle, you know."

"Yes, I know," said Emmy, "and my great-great-uncle, but did I ever meet him?"

"I doubt it. He wasn't much for family ties. Why, Jane Barmy and I were both his first cousins twice removed, but he never took notice of that. He was a widower, you know, and then once his daughter died, the only thing he took comfort in was his books."

Emmy considered the picture again. "He looks sad," she said quietly. "All his money didn't make him happy, either."

Mrs. Brecksniff lifted her hand, hesitated a moment, and then patted Emmy awkwardly on the shoulder. "Don't pay any attention to what Miss Barmy says. You're a good girl, Emmy. Maggie and I both know it, though we don't often tell you."

A warm feeling blossomed somewhere beneath Emmy's collarbone. She had had friends in this house all along.

There was a slight sound of skittering in the ceiling. Mrs. Brecksniff looked up with a frown. "Oh no—I'll have to call the exterminator again."

"I think it was just Maggie," said Emmy quickly as the housemaid came clattering down the stairs with a tray of tea things.

"Oh, Emmy, Miss Barmy is . . . indisposed," Maggie said, stopping. "She told me that she has arranged for a replacement nanny, a gentleman."

Emmy thought it best to look surprised.

Maggie shrugged. "She said that he would look after you during the party, and tell you when to go to the microphone, and so forth."

"What's wrong with Miss Barmy?" Emmy asked innocently.

Maggie giggled and glanced at Mrs. Brecksniff, who looked as if she were trying to keep a straight face.

"Gas," Mrs. Brecksniff said.

"Very bad gas," added Maggie.

"You might even say lethal," said the housekeeper, snorting. "Oh, dear me, there's the caterer at the door, and it's not even five o'clock!"

The Rat put his pencil down with a click. He was surrounded by crumpled pieces of paper, and he looked
hot and tired. Emmy, finishing up the sandwich she
had brought to her room, crushed the Rat's peanut-
butter-cup wrapper and threw it in the wastebasket.

"Ratty."

The Rat frowned. "Hush."

"Ratty, you don't have to sing."

The Rat shut his eyes. "Quiet," he said, waving her
away. "I'm getting something—it's coming— "

Emmy shook her head. How did he think he was
going to do it? Did he really imagine someone was
just going to announce that a singing rodent was on
the program and give him a microphone?

The Rat lifted his head suddenly. "I've got it!" he
cried. He pulled a fresh sheet of paper toward him,
sharpened the pencil with his teeth, and began scrib-
bling madly.

It was time to dress for the party. Emmy sighed as
she looked in the mirror, wishing that someone
would help her do her hair. It was hard to get the ribbons straight by herself.

Oh, well, it didn't matter. She was probably *supposed* to look like a neglected child tonight.

Emmy stared over the banister. She couldn't see the professor anywhere.

The large entry hall below was full of people, the women giving little shrieks of recognition, the men slapping backs and shaking hands. The air was perfumed with flowers and the hot scent of candles, and from the large reception room Emmy could hear strings—cellos, violins, the music like a warm pulse through the crowd.

Where were her parents? Emmy scanned the heads of those below. Of course it would probably be weeks before the chinchilla effect wore off naturally, but it was hard not to hope that this time would be different.

Emmy walked among elbows and chests, starched white shirtfronts, low-cut evening gowns and jewelry that dazzled the eye. The guests were all talking at once, and as Emmy moved through the crowd, fragments of their conversation came to her in spurts, like the voices on a radio when someone keeps turning the dial.

"It's fabulous, the latest thing, you've absolutely *got* to buy one—"

". . . so I dropped a hundred grand on a '53 Aston Martin DB35, completely rebuilt—"

". . . and did you hear the latest about Caroline? She actually—oh, *hello*, Caroline! Love the dress! Have you lost *weight*?"

Emmy threaded her way through narrow gaps between bodies and surged with the crowd past the double doors to the reception hall. At one end was a raised platform where a string quartet played valiantly against the tide of voices.

She waded to the platform and stepped up, standing on tiptoe for a better view. There was her father, by the door, talking loudly with a drink in his hand. She caught the word "Alaska."

"It took him three *hours* to do my hair, I thought I'd go *mad*, but of course he's worth every penny . . ."

It was her mother's voice, behind her. Emmy, feeling very low, didn't bother to turn around.

A side door swung open. Professor Capybara, sporting a red spotted bow tie, emerged from the kitchen and moved easily among the crowd, smiling, talking, gesturing. He was followed by a young and bearded waiter who carried a tray of pastries.

Emmy jumped down from the platform and moved purposefully toward him as the torrent of conversation swirled and eddied above her head.

"I know this is for some charity or the other, but honestly, I can't think which one, they all just *blur* in my mind—"

"Something about saving the children—or is it the whales?"

"Speaking of children, who's got ours tonight?" a man said carelessly.

"Oh, some babysitter . . . or wait, maybe they're sleeping over with friends." A woman in a beaded dress spoke vaguely. "Anyway, don't worry, darling, they're with *somebody*."

Emmy saw the professor through a space between elbows. She wedged in closer, coming up behind him.

"That's right—Hamelin jam tarts." The professor's voice was pitched above the noise. "Baked fresh this morning in Germany—see the little rat foot stamp? That's their signature imprint."

Little shrieks went up all around. Hands reached out to take the tarts from the silver tray that Brian offered.

"Oh, this is too *much*—a rat's foot, look at this!"

"Hamelin—isn't that the town in the story about the Pied Piper?"

"How clever of you," said the professor, beaming. "That is exactly right."

"Wasn't that the story about the guy who got rid of the rats and then got rid of the children?"

"What a *coincidence*—and this *fund-raiser* is for children—"

"Not a coincidence at all, ma'am," said the professor. "The Addisons had these specially made just for this event, because of the connection to lost and abandoned children, you see."

Emmy hid a grin and tugged on his sleeve. "Professor? Where did you leave the you-know-what?"

He inclined his head, dimpling beneath his beard. "Kitchen pantry," he said in her ear. "Blue case. I'll meet you upstairs in ten minutes."

21

THE CHINCHILLA was a little slow on the uptake.

"Jam is not brown," it said, licking boysenberry from between its toes. "It is not white with green things on top, either."

"This is not jam," Emmy explained patiently. "It's liverwurst. And the other one is cream cheese with olive."

The chinchilla peered dully at the little sandwiches before it. "But I like *jam*."

Emmy sighed, grasped the chinchilla firmly around its soft, tubby middle, and stamped its paw in the liverwurst. She stamped it in the cream cheese. Then she stamped it in a tofu canapé for good measure, covered the little sandwiches with a slice of thin cocktail bread, and speared each one with pickle and olive on toothpicks.

"There!" she said, dumping the chinchilla back in its cage with relief. She arranged the sandwiches on a tray along with two jam tarts and a cluster of grapes.

"I could have put my foot in the tarts, too," the chinchilla said, gazing at Emmy with its pale stupid eyes. "I like—"

"Jam," finished Emmy wearily. "I know." She washed the jam off the little clay sculpture she had baked earlier in the day and put it back in her pocket. "I'll wash off your foot, too, if you like."

The chinchilla, which had begun to lick its paw, stopped to consider this. "But I *like* liverwurst."

Professor Capybara was waiting in the third-floor hallway. Emmy walked carefully to Miss Barmy's door, holding the tray. The professor knocked.

"Why, Emmaline!" Miss Barmy's face looked blotchy and her eyes puffy, but she stretched her lips in a smile. "How very nice to see—"

She stopped dead and looked nervously behind her, sniffing the air. "I mean, it was very kind of you to bring me some food from the party."

"Professor Capybara thought it would be a good idea." Emmy held the tray out stiffly, in the manner of a reluctant child.

Miss Barmy's eyes glittered from Emmy to the professor. "Won't you come in?"

Emmy set the tray down on a little table. "It's for you," she said. "I already ate downstairs."

"But have you had one of these delicious-looking tarts?" Miss Barmy's smile widened.

"Professor Capybara said I couldn't have one without your permission." Emmy gazed up at her innocently. "They're full of refined sugar; they're terribly unhealthy."

"Pish posh!" Miss Barmy waved her hand airily. "Just one won't hurt you. Eat it, Emmaline—I insist."

"Really?" Emmy looked down at the tarts, each one with its rodent footprint in the exact center, and took one. "*Mmm!* They *are* good. Aren't you going to have a tart, too?"

Miss Barmy pushed the remaining tart to one side. "I think not, my dear. But I will try these charming little sandwiches." She took a dainty bite of the liverwurst, and then another, watching Emmy the whole time.

Emmy sat still for a moment. And then suddenly Miss Barmy began to smile.

It was a real smile this time, and it made her blotchy face quite extraordinarily beautiful. "You know, you really are a nice little girl," she said warmly. "And I'm afraid I've been rather horrible to you. I can't imagine why."

"Can't you?" said the professor, looking intensely interested.

Miss Barmy paused a moment, puzzled. "No, I can't. And it troubles me." Her eyes fell on her cane and she picked it up, touching the carved faces gently. "These were all nice girls, too."

"*Were*, Miss Barmy?" Emmy held her breath. "Are they dead?"

"No . . . no, I don't think so. It's their parents who are dead, but I can't quite remember why . . ."

"You're not feeling well, and we really must leave you in peace," said the professor as he ushered Emmy quickly out of the room. "More questions might be dangerous in her state," he added in a low voice.

"Must you go? There's really nothing wrong with me . . . nothing at all . . ."

A full, rounded, remarkably ripe and rotten smell came drifting out of the room like a cloud of poison gas. Emmy choked and ran for her room, followed by Professor Capybara, who was pinching his nose.

"Oh, help," he gasped as Emmy's door shut behind him. "I never would have believed it if I hadn't smelled it for myself."

Emmy pulled the clay model of a chinchilla foot out of her pocket and looked at it with satisfaction. "My idea worked pretty well, don't you think?"

"To perfection," said the professor, shaking her hand in congratulations. "You ate the fake chinchilla print, Miss Barmy the real—and now she's the one who's had her true values turned inside out!" He chortled happily, but sobered almost at once. "Still, you've only bought yourself some time. As soon as the chinchilla effect wears off, she'll be back to her normal self."

"When will that be, do you think?"

The professor pursed his lips. "It took a weekend to wear off for your parents the first time, didn't you say?"

Emmy nodded.

"Well, I'd guess Miss Barmy will be pleasant for at least that long. You see, the chinchilla effect varies depending on the strength of the principles it opposes. Your parents loved you, so they fought off the chinchilla effect very quickly—at least until it began to build up in their systems. Now, in Miss

Barmy's case, the badness in her will be battling the chinchilla effect for all it's worth."

"It'll be a short fight," said Emmy gloomily.

"Still, I'd be surprised if we didn't have at least a week of sweetness and light from the lady."

There was a rustling from within Emmy's bathroom and a small gray rodent came hurrying out, his hair spiky with gel. "Professor," the Rat cried breathlessly, clutching a bit of paper in his paw. "Is it time?"

"It's almost time for the program, if that's what you mean," said the professor, looking at his watch. "Emmy, shall we go? Let's show those people downstairs a real, live child—someone who should *not* be abandoned."

"But what about *me*?" The Rat jumped up and down, waving his paper. "I'm going to *sing*! I've got it all *ready*!"

The professor looked at him keenly. "I didn't know you wanted to be part of the program, Raston. I did bring the Universal Rodent Translator, but I was just going to let the chinchilla say a few words. That always impresses everyone."

The Rat looked appalled. "The chinchilla? You can't be serious!"

"I admit, he's not the brightest bulb in the light fixture—"

"He's as dumb as toast," said the Rat earnestly. "Look, it's all written down, it rhymes and everything, I spent *hours*—"

Professor Capybara tucked Raston into his breast pocket. "Come along then, Emmy," he said. "The program is about to start."

"But are you really going to let Raston sing?"

"Of course. Who could resist a singing rat?"

Professor Capybara moved briskly down the stairs and through the tiled hall. Surprised, Emmy noticed that people stepped aside as they approached, courteously letting them pass.

Snatches of conversation flew over her head as before. But there wasn't quite so much shrieking. The laughter was gentler, somehow. And the comments didn't seem nearly so mean.

"So how are your kids doing? Abby's about to graduate, isn't that right?"

". . . and the profits have been so good this year, I want to give employee bonuses."

"Sure, we made a small donation to S.P.A.N.K.—but I spent thirty times that on a dress for tonight. What was I *thinking*?"

They were at the platform. Emmy looked around, perplexed.

"Say, where *are* our kids tonight?" A dark-haired man set down his drink, frowning, and turned to a woman wearing a dress of silver beads.

She stared at him, her eyes wide. "John! I just realized—I have *no idea!*"

"Testing, testing," said the professor, tapping a microphone that was affixed to a tall wooden stand. He spoke quietly to Emmy's mother. The musicians put down their bows as Mrs. Addison stepped to the wooden lectern and laid down a sheet of paper.

"Darlings," she trilled. "Thank you *so* much for coming tonight to this fund-raiser for the"—she looked down at the paper—"for the Society for the Protection of Abandoned and Neglected Kids. My daughter, Emmy, is here to remind us of the real children we are trying to help."

Emmy stepped up on a little box and leaned over the lectern. "Hello," she said shyly, into the microphone.

"And as a further treat, we have here a surprise visit from the very distinguished Maxwell Capybara, world-renowned professor of rodentology, who has come with something very *unusual* for us tonight. Professor?"

"Thank you, Mrs. Addison. Some years ago, I retired to do further research into the wonderful and amazing abilities of rodents. And here tonight, for the benefit of abandoned and neglected children everywhere, you are about to witness the world premiere of one of the most amazing rodents it has been my privilege to know. Please give your closest attention to the astounding, the extraordinary, the incredible shrinking Raston Rat!"

The lights dimmed. A spotlight shone as the professor affixed a small metal box to the microphone's head, lifted Raston from his pocket, and set him on top of the lectern.

The Rat pulled out his paper, somewhat crumpled, and cleared his throat. He blinked in the bright light, looked out over the crowd—and froze.

There was a profound silence. From a ceiling vent overhead came a small restless shuffling.

"Sing!" Emmy hissed, poking him lightly in the back.

The Rat blushed from his ears to his tail, took a deep, chest-swelling breath, and sang. To the tune of "The Star-Spangled Banner," he sang, with all the power his lungs possessed:

Oh, say have you seen
The kiddies forlorn
Who have truckloads of toys
But still need our pity?
Though they've got gobs of cash
Though they're dressed, oh so fash—
They're all grumpy and glum
And in short, it's not pretty.
They've got no time to play
'Cause they're scheduled all day
And when they get home
Everyone is away.
Oh, who are these abandoned,
Neglected children, sad and lone?
My dear S.P.A.N.K.ers, one and all—
They just might be your own!

There was a pause. From the vent overhead came an enthusiastic squeak. And then the room erupted in a thunder of applause.

The dark-haired man put his arm around his wife,

and together they turned toward the door. "Sorry—excuse us—we have to find our children," Emmy heard as they walked rapidly out.

There was a sound of sniffling. All around the room, eyes were dabbed and noses were honked. Emmy looked at her parents, standing together and staring. And then the professor was at her side, tucking Raston into his pocket.

"One of the best appeals I've ever heard," he said, chuckling to himself as he led Emmy out of the room, "and certainly the most creative. Raston, you're a *star.*"

Emmy looked over her shoulder at the partygoers as she followed the professor up the stairs. "They're all so different now," she marveled. "I still can't believe you imprinted all those tarts and handed them around."

"It wasn't in the original plan," the professor admitted, "but when I listened a moment to the talk at the party, I couldn't resist. Somebody had to wake up those people."

"What do you mean?" The Rat poked his head out of the professor's pocket. "I did that with my song, didn't I?"

Professor Capybara nodded. "Yes, indeed. But they wouldn't have bothered to listen if the tarts hadn't prepared the way. Brian and I didn't go near your parents, of course," he added hastily, looking at Emmy. "But to all the rest of them—all those shallow, bragging, vulgar folk—we gave the chinchilla tarts. All at once, the things they thought were important became petty and small. And the things they didn't care much about were suddenly worth the whole world."

Emmy smiled.

"So you mean—," said the Rat, light dawning.

The professor chuckled deep in his chest. "That's right! Suddenly, money meant *nothing* to them, except for the good it could do. They no longer cared about trying to make people envy them—they thought about making people feel valued. And their children, who they had neglected and forgotten and left to the care of strangers—"

"Became the most important people in the world!" finished the Rat triumphantly.

"It may not last, of course," said the professor, sighing, "at least not for most of them. But it's a nice change, don't you think?"

Emmy nodded fervently as she mounted the last flight of stairs. "Speaking of change, Professor, Miss Barmy isn't going to stay nice for long. Would you try very hard tomorrow to find a rat potion that will stop her for good?"

"Yes, I certainly shall." Professor Capybara puffed slightly as he reached the third-floor hall. "But the chart, as you know, is smudged and faint in some very crucial places; and my notes are completely mixed up. I don't even have a blood sample to analyze."

"A blood sample? From Miss Barmy?"

"Yes. That's where the charascope is so useful, you see. It shows me all of her weak points."

A door opened at the end of the hall. Miss Barmy shuffled toward the bathroom wearing a fluffy white robe and bunny slippers.

"Why, hello!" she cried gaily, moving to Emmy with her hands outstretched. "I'm so *glad* to see you!"

Emmy smiled back, feeling a painful twist somewhere inside of her. So this is what Miss Barmy could have been like . . . warm and lovely and welcoming. She shook her head suddenly, to clear it. Miss Barmy was *not* like this, but for the moment, Emmy could take advantage of it.

"Miss Barmy," she said gently, "I need a few blood samples for a science project. Would you . . . could you—"

"Of course," said Miss Barmy. "Take as much as you like."

"I'll get my notes organized first thing tomorrow." The professor, on his knees in Emmy's room, was peering down the heat vent. Brian, still in his waiter's jacket, rubbed his bearded chin as a skittering sound of many small feet echoed in the wall.

Joe and the rodents tumbled out of the heat vent, already cheering.

"Hooray for Raston!"

"Ratty forever!"

"Oh, Rasty," cried Sissy, "you're a poet and I didn't even know it!"

The Rat was surrounded by a hugging, congratulating mob. He swayed under the press, his mouth open in a foolish, ecstatic grin, his ears twitching at each compliment. Emmy watched, trying not to laugh.

"And so Raston finally gets what he's been craving all along," said the professor, smiling.

Brian cleared his throat. "And when will the other rodents get what they want?" he asked unhappily.

Emmy glanced at him in surprise. "What's the matter?"

Brian looked away. "It's the rats," he muttered. "Ever since Raston bit me, I can understand everything they say. And they want to get out!" he added emphatically, raising his eyes. "They can't stand it in those cages!"

"Soon," said the professor earnestly. "But you know the police searched the Antique Rat today, looking for clues, trying to find Joe. They saw all the rats in their cages, and if they come back and suddenly all the rats are gone, it will seem even more suspicious."

Brian slumped in his chair.

"Once Joe grows and returns to his parents, then we can set them free. But it's not safe yet."

"I talked to Uncle Cheswick." Brian wound the tip of his beard around a finger. "If you just let him grow, he promises to never let Miss Barmy use the rodents again."

Emmy and the professor exchanged glances.

"Why do you care so much about Cheswick Vole?" asked the professor gently.

"He's my *uncle*," said Brian with dignity, "and he took me out of the orphanage." He got to his feet. "I'll go put the chinchilla in the truck. But what about the other potions we let Miss Barmy have—the Oil of Beaver and the Extract of Gerbil? Now that she's nicer, we could ask for them back—"

There was a sudden clatter as the vent cover dropped from the professor's hands.

"What did you say?" Professor Capybara's face had turned pale. "You gave her Extract of *Gerbil*? Not—triple distilled?"

"We thought it was safe enough," said Emmy anxiously. "It just makes you more mature. What's wrong, Professor?"

He gripped her arm. "It makes you more mature, all right," he said hoarsely. "It makes you age—" He paused, his grip loosening.

"Professor! Wake up!" Emmy shook him violently.

Professor Capybara's eyes popped open like a puppet's. "It makes you age . . . by a factor of three . . ."

he said in a thick, drowsy voice and sagged heavily to the floor, already snoring.

Emmy stared at the rumpled heap that was the professor. "If that's true," she said slowly, "then Miss Barmy *couldn't* have meant it for herself."

Brian looked at Emmy in horror. "But if Miss Barmy gave it to you—"

Emmy shuddered lightly, as if touched by a chill breeze.

"—you'd be over thirty years old," Brian whispered.

The attempt to get the Extract of Gerbil from Miss Barmy had been unsuccessful. Her door was locked, and all their knocking had failed to rouse her.

The professor woke at last, but he was still so upset he kept falling asleep again. Emmy helped Brian get him into the truck.

"Don't be afraid," said Brian, his worried eyes on her face. "I've got Miss Barmy's blood sample right here. Tomorrow I'll help the professor go through all his notes, and look at that chart in a good light, and . . . and I'll keep him calm. We'll figure something out for sure."

Emmy nodded. Her teeth were chattering slightly in the cool night air.

"Besides," Brian went on with an attempt at a smile, "Miss Barmy's going to stay nice for days, right? And why would she want to make you into a grown-up anyway? It doesn't make sense."

Emmy rubbed the goose pimples on her arms. She'd always thought it would be wonderful to be a grown-up—but not all at once. Not if she had to miss everything in between.

Brian slammed the truck door and leaned out through the open window, still looking unhappy. "I'd feel better if your parents cared enough to listen to you a little. Could you get them to take you along when they leave town? Keep you out of Miss Barmy's way?"

Emmy shrugged. "Maybe."

"They wouldn't have to care a lot," he went on, thinking aloud. "I mean, at the orphanage there wasn't anybody who loved me the way a parent would, but some of the staff were fond of me. Emmy, if your parents were even just *fond* of you, they might listen enough to keep you safe."

On her way up to bed, Emmy stopped at her parents' room.

"Mom?" She hesitated in the doorway. "Are you going to stay home for a while, or are you planning another trip soon?"

Her mother looked up languidly from her dressing table and dipped two fingers in a jar of cold cream. "Oh, another trip, naturally, though what I'll do in Alaska I can't imagine. I'm not sloshing about with any big clammy fish, I can tell you *that*." She applied the cream to her face with a careful, circular motion.

"You could take me with you," said Emmy, wandering over to the chest of drawers. She poked at a tube of wrinkle remover and gazed idly at the bottles of nail polish cluttering the surface, along with her mother's silver brush and comb set.

Her mother looked blank. "Take you with us? Whatever for?"

"Well, while Dad's fishing, you and I could do something together." Emmy thought rapidly. "Shopping, maybe?"

"Shopping? In *Alaska*?" Kathy Addison gave a tinkling laugh. "What would we buy? A stuffed moose?"

Emmy said nothing. She was staring at the dresser top. Her mother's brush was on the left, her father's on the right . . .

Kathy Addison waved airily. "Don't talk nonsense, of course you can't come. We'll be going straight to Rome from there. I'm simply *dying* to see Count Zippoli and his dancing ferrets—"

I'm not going to use the Endear Mouse anyway, Emmy told herself, looking at the strands of her parents' hair tangled in the brushes.

"—and don't you have school, or something? You're in what grade now? Fourth? Sixth?"

But just in case, Emmy thought.

"—and then we've been invited to the Transylvanian Vampire's Ball, and that's hardly an event for children—"

It's silly to take them, Emmy said to herself, even as her hand quietly extracted one hair from each brush and folded them in a tissue. It's not like I'll ever really *use* them. I'll probably forget I even have them in my pocket.

EMMY WAS EATING BREAKFAST in the kitchen when the news came on.

"Don't tell me they haven't found that boy yet," said Maggie, her eyes troubled. "He's been missing, what—two days now?"

Emmy nodded, her eyes never leaving the screen. Studley Jackell was having better luck this time—Joe's parents weren't trying to shut the door in his face. Mrs. Benson, pale and thin, was dabbing at her eyes with a handkerchief. Mr. Benson stood squarely in front of the microphone, looking grim and determined.

"And so young Joe Benson is still missing," said Studley Jackell, his voice deep and booming, "and his parents are still wondering, worrying, watching, waiting—"

"He's eleven," interrupted Mr. Benson, leaning into the microphone, "about four feet ten inches tall with thick blond hair, wearing a blue soccer jersey—"

"That's right," said Studley, grabbing the microphone. "Joe Benson was an outstanding soccer player with hopes for the national junior team. His loss means bad news for Grayson Lake's tournament hopes—"

"What does *that* matter?" Mr. Benson's face darkened. "I don't care if Joe never plays soccer again. I just want my son back, safe at home."

"And so do we all," intoned Studley Jackell, smoothing back his hair and blocking Mr. Benson from the microphone in one practiced motion. "Monica, do the police have any leads?"

"Well, Studley, the police released Cheswick Vole since they had no real evidence to connect him to the disappearance of Joe Benson. But we have just been told that the police want him for questioning again—and he is nowhere to be found."

"It's a real mystery, isn't it, Monica."

"It certainly is, Studley. But there's nothing mysterious about the way Ron Ronson's Used Cars and Trucks saves you money!"

Maggie snapped off the TV. "I can't bear it," she said. "Those poor parents. And that poor boy."

"I bet Joe will turn up safe," said Emmy, pouring milk on her cereal. "He's probably having a great time somewhere and just forgot to go home."

"I shall pray for it," said Maggie simply, measuring coffee into a pot.

Emmy finished her cereal quickly. Joe would want to hear what was on the news, especially the part about how his father didn't care if he ever played soccer again.

She would take Ratty and Sissy with her, she thought, rinsing her bowl. They would pick up Joe at Rodent City and then go to see Brian and the professor. A magnifying glass would help them read the fine print on the chart, and maybe make some sense out of the smudged spots, too. With all of them working on the problem, surely they could come up with something that would keep her parents from flying to Alaska tonight.

There was a scraping sound in the hall, and a soft bump at the door. Emmy's fingers tightened on her spoon as she looked up—and then she met Miss Barmy's cheery smile.

"What a lovely Saturday morning! Doesn't the sunshine just make you feel lucky to be alive?"

"I'm telling you, it's weird." Emmy stared out the window of the Antique Rat. On the far side of the green, Mr. Bee whittled peacefully in his doorway, ducking occasionally as his wife threw another flowerpot.

"What?" Joe sprawled on the desk blotter, doodling with a broken bit of pencil. Nearby, Professor Capybara peered through the charascope, making notations on a small yellow pad.

"I *know* what Miss Barmy's done to me," Emmy said moodily, "but when she acts so nice, I almost forget how nasty she really is."

"Dangerous," said the professor at once, looking up. "Terribly dangerous, as her blood sample proves. Look here."

Emmy bent over the charascope as the professor slid a small rectangle of glass under the lens. The glowing bits she remembered swam in bright crystal patterns, replicating and splitting in a lively tumble of changing shapes. "I don't get it. That looks just like the sample of your blood I saw before."

"It *is* my blood. Now look at this one, and compare."

Professor Capybara replaced the slide with another and Emmy looked through the eyepiece, blinking in surprise. The glowing brightness had become something murkier, like pond water seen several feet below the surface. The gleaming bits were still there, flipping and changing as she watched, but there was a dark edge to the patterns, and the shapes looked oddly distorted.

"Let me see," said Joe, and Emmy lifted him to the top of the charascope, where he stood on a brass fitting and put his whole head in the left eyecup.

"Criminy! Look at the ball of nightcrawlers!"

"What?" Emmy turned quickly. "Where?"

"It just swam into view." Joe swung out of the way as Emmy slid into the chair and bent her head.

The ball was still there, green and wriggling, made up of dark, twisted wormlike shapes. Emmy had seen one of them before, in the professor's blood; but this was a whole mass of them, writhing together. And as she watched, horrified, another worm cluster floated past, and then another.

She sat back, feeling sick.

"Not very pretty, is it?" The professor snapped off the light that illumined the slide and dusted off his hands. "We've all got a worm or two floating around, but let them linger and grow, and—well—that's what you get."

Emmy whirled the swivel chair so she faced away from the desk. She didn't want to waste one more minute thinking about Miss Barmy's stupid ball of resentments. "Come on, Joe," she said, putting out her hand for him to step up on. "Let's help Brian with the chart. Your little eyes will be perfect for close-up work."

Emmy walked quickly home for lunch. The sun was warm on her face and the blossoming trees filled the air with scent, but she hardly noticed. She was wondering what her own blood would look like under the charascope.

"Are we there yet?" The Rat, drowsing in the warmth of her shirt pocket, poked his nose out.

Emmy stroked his head lightly. "You should have gone with Sissy. You would have been eating lunch at Mrs. Bunjee's by now."

"Acorn soup," said the Rat with disdain. "That's not lunch, that's punishment."

"Maggie might not give me any peanut-butter cups, you know."

"Do your best," said the Rat cheerfully. "And put me on that vine below your window—I want to climb up and play on the train."

"But, Ratty—your ankle!"

"All better," said the Rat briskly. "We rodents heal rapidly. Besides, I have to get in shape for the next pawball game."

"But will they even let you play?"

The Rat's face split in a wide and ecstatic smile. "Chippy said I could—if I wrote the team song!"

A shadow appeared in the doorway as Emmy mounted the back steps.

"There you are, Emmaline, just in time for lunch!" Miss Barmy smiled broadly and opened the refrigerator to reveal a frosty glass. "I made a milkshake especially for you. It's delicious!"

Emmy stared at the creamy cold froth. Miss Barmy still seemed perfectly nice; it was unlikely that the milkshake contained Extract of Gerbil. And there was no explosive noise, no putrefying stench that would accompany a lie, so it must taste all right.

But Emmy wasn't going to take the risk. She hadn't forgotten the mass of green worms she had seen in the charascope.

"It's so *healthy*, Emmaline," said Miss Barmy, holding out the glass. "I've always wanted the very best for you, you know."

Emmy waited. A lie was a lie, no matter how much the person speaking might think it was true. . . .

But there was no smell at all. Emmy glanced up sharply. Surely the Oil of Beaver couldn't have worn off already?

"Really, I insist," said Miss Barmy. "Drink it."

Emmy's gaze traveled down from Miss Barmy's face to her fingers. Each of the nanny's fingers was bandaged. There was a strong smell of antibiotic ointment, and several of the fingers had bled through the gauze.

Miss Barmy must have scrubbed her fingers raw. And now there was no trace of Oil of Beaver left on her skin.

Emmy looked at Miss Barmy's smiling face and hooded eyes and saw that the professor had been wrong. The chinchilla effect was not going to last a week. It had not even lasted one day.

"I need to go," Emmy said suddenly, backing toward the door.

"No," Miss Barmy said, "you need to drink this. Now." Her hand made a convulsive movement and she gripped her cane.

Emmy pressed her hands against the screen door. "I'm going out. I want to—to play in the park."

Miss Barmy's breath came and went with a quick rise and fall of her chest. "You'll get dirty in the park."

"I want to get dirty!" said Emmy passionately. "I want to catch frogs and climb trees and—and build forts—"

"Besides, you have a tennis lesson in an hour." Miss Barmy's voice was thin. "And little theater and basket weaving after that."

"I take too many classes," said Emmy. "Do you know what I think?"

Miss Barmy's lip lifted in a slight sneer.

"I think that kids should have time to just play. On their own. With no grown-ups around, trying to organize them."

"Do you indeed?" Miss Barmy said softly. "Well"—she looked down, smoothing her palm over the top of her cane—"perhaps you are right."

Emmy narrowed her eyes. It couldn't be this easy. Standing up to Miss Barmy had never worked before.

Miss Barmy was still looking down. Emmy followed her gaze.

The nanny was stroking her cane, running her hand over the carved faces. Some of the blood from her fingertips left rust-colored streaks on the white, polished wood of the cane.

Watching, Emmy felt a chill. The tiny hairs on her arms lifted.

Miss Barmy, still looking down, smiled. "Yes, Emmaline. You *should* go to the park. Absolutely. Right now, if you like."

Emmy was out. Still a nagging uneasiness in the corner of her mind, vague and undefined, kept her from going too far away, and she kicked a stone along her street, thinking things through.

Should she spy on Miss Barmy? But what good would that do? Extract of Gerbil was taken in through the mouth, so as long as Emmy didn't eat or drink anything the nanny had touched, she would be safe. It wasn't that hard to go without lunch for once—and she could always make it up later.

She would go to the Antique Rat. Maybe the Professor and Brian and Joe had found something that would work on her parents.

Emmy tossed back her bangs, suddenly annoyed. She was tired of waiting for other people to find something that would work. All right, then, she would just do the chinchilla trick again. Maybe she could build niceness up in Miss Barmy's system, the same way Miss Barmy had built up the opposite in her parents!

Emmy trotted purposefully up the hill toward Main Street. It was a good plan, if temporary. In fact, she could just keep on using the chinchilla over and over until her parents came home from Alaska and Rome and wherever else they were going. It would mean weeks of strategy and careful timing, but it was better than stabbing the Endear Mouse in the heart.

A small blue car turned the corner ahead and came toward Emmy. She ducked behind a convenient hedge as it slowed down. She'd caught a glimpse of the driver through the window, and he looked suspiciously like Dr. Leander, the school psychologist. The last thing Emmy wanted was to get into another discussion about *problems*.

Dr. Leander stopped the car, unfolded a map, and looked vaguely around. Emmy shrank back into the shadow of the hedge. The polite thing to do would be to offer assistance, but Emmy already had to talk to him twice each month and that was more than enough. It wasn't easy to talk to someone who kept searching for signs of mental illness. And finding them, probably, thought Emmy with a little grin, remembering the last time.

Dr. Leander drove slowly on, down the hill and toward the lake. Emmy watched absently—until the car turned down her own driveway. And then the nagging, uneasy feeling that had been hanging over her sharpened, came to a point, and pricked her with a sense of clear and looming danger.

"WE HAD NO IDEA." Jim Addison's voice was subdued. He looked at his wife.

"No idea at all," echoed Kathy Addison. "None."

Emmy shut her eyes and tried to control her breathing. Soft, soft—in through the nose, out through the mouth—

She had run home, slipped quietly in the back door, and tiptoed through the house. The study door was open a crack; inside were her parents, Miss Barmy, and Dr. Leander.

"I didn't want to worry you," said Miss Barmy. "I thought I could control Emmaline's moods with a careful and healthful diet. And, too, I felt that Dr. Leander was keeping an eye on her at school. So I said nothing about the delusions, and the fits of temper, and the terrible rages—until last night, when I realized that she was a danger to herself—and to others."

Miss Barmy held up her hands with the fingertips wrapped in bloody gauze. Kathy Addison leaned forward in horror.

"Emmy did *that?*"

Miss Barmy nodded solemnly. "She bit them. All ten. She was like a wild animal."

Emmy stiffened in outrage, her eye to the crack.

There was a rustle of paper. "She may have thought you were the giant spider trying to suck out her brains," said the psychologist, consulting his notes. "Or—let's see—the ten-foot-tall noodle? Perhaps she was only defending herself. These delusions can be very real to a person who is mentally ill."

Emmy winced. What had she said to Dr. Leander? She could hardly remember—but the giant sucking spider *did* sound familiar.

"But what can we do?" Kathy Addison looked upset. "We're flying to Alaska tonight, or we'd be at her side every minute—"

Emmy sagged against the doorjamb. The chinchilla print wasn't wearing off early. It *couldn't* be, or her mother wouldn't talk about going away when she thought her daughter was ill.

"You don't need to worry about a thing." Miss Barmy spoke with firm authority. "I know just the place where she will be gently restrained and given the very best of care. And it's only temporary, you know. When you get back from your travels, you can visit her, and take her back home if you think it's the best thing to do."

"And what is this place, exactly?" Kathy Addison tapped her nails on the arm of her chair. "We only want the best for Emmy, you know."

"Coincidentally, one of the best institutions in the nation is right here in Grayson Lake. It's very exclusive, and very expensive."

"Well, if it's exclusive, it must be good," said Emmy's mother.

"Spare no expense!" boomed Jim Addison. "Emmy's got to have the best! I'll write the check right now!"

"Write it to the Home for Troubled Girls," said Miss Barmy promptly. "I'll get the commitment papers in order, and you can sign them this afternoon. By tonight, Emmaline will be taken care of, and you won't have to worry about her ever again." She paused. "Oh—and there's one more little thing."

Emmy trembled. The Home for Troubled Girls! There was a weakness in her knees, and a sick feeling in her stomach. She put a hand over her mouth.

"What if something should happen to you?" Miss Barmy's voice was solemn. "Do you have a will that appoints a guardian for Emmaline, and an executor for the estate?"

"Why, no, I don't believe we do," said Kathy Addison slowly. "Of course all our money would go to Emmy, but someone responsible would have to take care of it for her."

"We meant to write a will one of these days," said Emmy's father, "but we just never got around to it."

"If you like," said Miss Barmy casually, looking at her nails, "we can take care of that this afternoon, too. I know a lawyer who would be happy to draw up the papers. Have you thought about who you might like to appoint as guardian?"

"Why, you, I suppose, Miss Barmy," said Kathy Addison. "We don't really have any other relatives, to speak of."

"A wise choice," said Dr. Leander, "given Emmy's precarious mental state. Miss Barmy has been very concerned about Emmy this past year. I can assure you that she will be an excellent guardian."

"We might as well do it right," said Jim Addison heartily, "and make Miss Barmy trustee, too. Bring that lawyer, and we'll take care of business this afternoon. Make it before six o'clock, though." He looked at his watch. "We've got a flight to catch."

Emmy backed slowly away from the study door. With shaking hands, she found the wall and climbed the stairs blindly.

What now?

There was a shuffle of feet in the foyer and the sound of voices. Emmy pressed against the wall, trembling with anger. They were going to get rid of her—like they would a dog that chewed the carpet!

As if she had felt Emmy's fierce gaze, Miss Barmy looked up. Emmy whirled up the second flight of stairs, dashed into her room, and wedged a chair under her doorknob.

There. At least Miss Barmy couldn't barge in on her while she was trying to think what to do.

Muffled footsteps sounded on the stairs and progressed firmly toward Emmy's room, with every so often a thunking sound, out of rhythm. Emmy backed away from the door, not breathing.

There was a sound of metal sliding on metal, and the doorknob gave a soft click. The footsteps started up again, got fainter, went away.

Emmy waited a moment. Then she slid the chair away, grasped the doorknob, and twisted. But it wouldn't turn.

She had been locked in her room.

Emmy paced the floor, her cheeks hot and her eyes dry. Unless she did something fast, Miss Barmy was going to have her locked up and put away where even her friends couldn't find her.

Worse yet, Emmy's parents were going to name Miss Barmy as Emmy's legal guardian and the trustee of the estate. So if Kathy and Jim Addison died—or disappeared—not only would Emmy be under Miss Barmy's control, but the entire Addison fortune would be as well.

What was it Mrs. Brecksniff had said once? That all Miss Barmy cared about was the Addison money?

Emmy shivered. Once those papers were signed, the only thing that would keep Miss Barmy from the money she wanted would be the fact that Emmy's parents were still alive.

Still . . . alive. . . . The words hung in Emmy's mind, as if waiting for her to understand. And then all at once she did.

The Extract of Gerbil had not been meant for her at all. It had been meant for her parents. Kathy and Jim Addison, aged 35 and 37, respectively, would become . . .

Emmy's mouth went dry as she did the math.

Twenty-four hours after Miss Barmy slipped them the extract, her parents would be 105 and 111. Tomorrow, somewhere in Alaska, two very elderly people would die among strangers.

There was a soft sound of scampering feet. The Endear Mouse ran out from the playroom, up Emmy's leg, and onto her knee.

"What's wrong?" The question was posed simply, mind to mind.

Emmy bent her head down, near the mouse. It moved under the curtain of her hair to touch her cheek. And she was not surprised when, after a while, the Endear Mouse ran under the bed. It was all too much for such a little creature. . . .

It was too much for Emmy.

She stepped into her bathroom, washed out the soap dish, and dried it. Then she groped in the back pocket of her jeans and pulled out a neatly folded tissue.

She was having trouble seeing clearly. She wiped the back of her hand across her eyes and dried her hand on her jeans before she laid the strands of her parents' hair carefully in the shallow dish. She glanced in the mirror and then quickly away. Should she call the mouse? Would she have to catch it?

There was a tug on her sock. Emmy bent down to see the Endear Mouse dragging what looked like a bit of paper. . . . It was the instruction tag. Taped inside was the sharp, hollow needle.

The Endear Mouse looked up at her with eyes that were bright and steady, and pressed its paw to her ankle. "Go ahead, Emmy," came the thought, small and brave. "My heart is strong."

The tiny mouse stepped into her lowered hand. Its paws were white, its tail neatly curled, and its fur was so light that Emmy's breath stirred it. She looked down at the small bit of life cupped in her palm and positioned the needle against its beating heart.

And then—

And then she couldn't do it. She was going to have to do something else to rescue her parents, because as it turned out, she wasn't a murderer.

Emmy realized this fact with some relief. She threw the needle into the toilet along with the instruction tag and flushed. The Endear Mouse leaped from her hand and clawed its way up to the top of her head, trembling violently.

"What's this?" Emmy gently lifted the mouse out of her hair, disengaging the little claws that dug into her scalp. "You wanted me to stick a needle into your heart but you're scared of a flushing toilet?"

The Endear Mouse hid its head. Emmy laughed softly.

"You're awfully brave," she whispered in its ear. "If I were your size, I'd be afraid of a toilet, too."

"So what do we do now?" Emmy lay on the floor of the playroom, her chin propped up on her forearms, and stared into the dollhouse. The Endear Mouse, tired out, was asleep in the attic. The Rat, rumpled but awake, looked thoughtful.

"First thing, we need to get you out of here before they put you away. If you were my size, it'd be easy," said the Rat, climbing out of the dollhouse. "But as big as you are—"

He stopped. Emmy turned.

There was a tiny sound of metal on metal. There was a click from the doorknob. And then there were footsteps inside Emmy's room.

"Quick, Ratty," whispered Emmy, hunkering down to the floor. "Shrink me."

The Rat looked at her, alarmed. "But it's the third bite—we don't know what will happen!"

"But I'm full size again. Just do it!" Emmy said, nearly sick with dread—and the Rat did.

It felt the same as before. Emmy shut up just like a telescope, going down like a very fast elevator. It was with intense relief that she saw she was no smaller than the Rat—and still herself, and fully visible.

"Quick! Over here!" Raston beckoned with his paw, and Emmy scuttled underneath a chest. She kicked up a dust ball in her path and sneezed.

Footsteps shook the floor. Emmy felt the vibration throughout her body. Step, step, clunk. Step, step, clunk. Miss Barmy's cane made a bone-jarring thud.

"Emmaline." The voice was pitched low. Emmy shrank back farther beneath the chest, hugging her shoulders.

"Come out, come out, wherever you are," sang Miss Barmy in a playful tone. "Time for nice little girls to go somewhere special."

Emmy backed up farther, shuddering. She couldn't get far enough away from this evil woman. Back, back, into the dark—

"*Ouch!*" yelped the Rat as she stepped on his tail.

"Who said that?" cried Miss Barmy. The metal-tipped shoes came closer, closer—and stopped. There was a listening silence.

Emmy's dread was suddenly crowded out by an idea. A big idea that came to her all at once, complete and inspired.

"Ratty," she whispered in his ear, "say something else. Say it *loud.*"

The Rat's eyes reflected yellow in the dark. "Are you *insane?*"

"Just do it!" hissed Emmy, and the Rat obeyed.

"GET LOST, BARMY BABY!" he screamed.

The words rang, echoing from wall to wall. Miss Barmy's feet came closer. Her knees touched the floor—her hands—and last of all, the nanny laid her cheek on the rug and peered under the toy chest, her eyes searching the shadows.

"Emmaline." Miss Barmy's voice was calm, soothing. "You don't really want me to get lost. You want me to *find* you. And I'm close—yes, I'm very *close* to finding you—"

She reached a hand beneath the toy chest. The huge fingers, bloody, gauze wrapped, came nearer, wiggling, probing—

"Now!" whispered Emmy in the Rat's ear. "Bite her, Ratty!"

"No way!" Raston's whisper was agitated. "The first bite won't shrink her, and I'll never get a second bite in before she goes after me with a broom, or her shoe, or something—"

Emmy groaned. "Do it NOW!" She slapped him on the rump.

The Rat, startled, leaped forward with his mouth open, collided with Miss Barmy's index finger—and bit down, hard.

Miss Barmy let out a sound like a train whistle, loud, high, and piercing.

And then she shrank.

"Grab her!" yelled Emmy. "Hold her down!"

"But that was just the first bite!" protested the Rat, scrambling after Miss Barmy. He caught her easily and held her against the floor, struggling and kicking.

Emmy came running with a shoelace. "You hold that end," she said briefly. "Here—wind it around her legs—"

"I'll get you for this!" screeched Miss Barmy. "You'll never get away with it—you vicious little *worm*—"

"Pull her arms back tight," directed Emmy. "That's right—now over her mouth."

The Rat's paws moved nimbly through a series of intricate knots. "I'm glad all those Scout meetings in Herbifore's room were good for something," he muttered. "Let's see—square knot, half hitch, bowline . . ."

Miss Barmy's shouts were muffled as the shoelace effectively gagged her. The Rat tied a last firm knot and sat down, scratching his head.

"I don't get it," he mumbled. "How come she shrank with the first bite?"

"She answered you back, remember?" Emmy leaned forward. "That's when I knew—if she could understand rat speech, you must have bitten her once already!"

"Never," said the Rat, making a face. "She tasted awful. I would have remembered."

"Maybe you were too little to remember." Emmy began to pace, thinking aloud. "Maybe it happened long ago, when Cheswick Vole first brought the rodents to Grayson Lake. Maybe—"

Miss Barmy lay perfectly still. Her eyes glittered.

"Is that true, Miss Barmy?" Emmy stood over her. "Is *that* when Raston bit you? Were you *helping* Cheswick steal the rats?"

"O wahih eye wah!" said Miss Barmy.

Emmy loosened the gag.

"So what if I was?" repeated Miss Barmy belligerently. "I was only trying to get what was due to me. I only wanted what should have been mine!"

"What was that?" asked the Rat, curiously.

"This house! The Addison fortune!" She glared at Emmy. "Old William may have been your great-great-uncle, but he was *my* first cousin twice removed. My *mother* was an Addison . . . she was old William's *housekeeper*—"

"I never heard that," the Rat said.

"I grew up in this house, but unlike William's daughter, I had to work. For years I had to be a nanny to other rich little girls. I *hate* rich little girls!" she cried, her face growing purple with fury. "But I never forgot I was an Addison. I never forgot that this should have been *my* house, *my* money . . . ."

Jane Barmy tossed back the hair that hung wild about her face. "I came back after Cheswick told me about the rats. When old William's daughter drowned, I took care of him . . . ."

Emmy shuddered.

Miss Barmy continued, a mad light in her eyes. "I tried Essence of Hamster and Lemming Drops and Prairie Dog Pus on him. I thought I had done enough, but then he left everything to your parents! To *you*!"

Emmy felt sick. Her eyes fell on Miss Barmy's cane, which had clattered to the floor when she shrank. The carved faces looked more pleading than usual, and Emmy swallowed, avoiding their gaze. Was one of them old William? There was a blank spot that had been meant for Emmy's face someday, she knew. . . .

A sleepy Endear Mouse poked its head out of the dollhouse attic at a sudden noise of chattering from the windowsill, followed by several thumps and the sound of scurrying feet. Chippy, Buck, Mrs. Bunjee, Sissy, and Joe skidded into the playroom—and stopped dead at the sight of a tiny Miss Barmy, tied up with a shoelace.

"Well, well," said Joe. "*This* is an interesting development."

24

"So you're still in danger, then, Emmy," Buck said soberly.

Emmy nodded, looking around the circle at the serious faces of her friends. "My parents are going to sign papers with the lawyer this afternoon, and then they're leaving town. So even if Miss Barmy's not around—"

"Emmy could be locked up by suppertime," said the Rat grimly.

"Not if she stays little," said Chippy.

No one said anything for a moment. Emmy soothed the Endear Mouse, who had run to her.

"She could live with us in Rodent City," said Buck. "Couldn't she, Mother?"

Mrs. Bunjee shook her head. "A visit is one thing, but she can't stay little forever, and neither can Joe. His parents must be sick with worry," she added severely, looking at him over her whiskers. "Pawball is all well and good, but it shouldn't come between children and their parents."

Joe looked abashed.

"There's one more thing," said Emmy, feeling her stomach tighten as she looked at Miss Barmy. "Where is the Extract of Gerbil?"

"Wouldn't you like to know?" Miss Barmy's face was lumpy with spite. "It might be hidden away where you'll never find it. Or it might already be in the food your parents are going to eat tonight . . . or their toothpaste, or their water glass, or their breath mints."

Rage and fear surged in Emmy like a river rising. As she struggled for control, she knew exactly what her blood would look like under the charascope now.

Mrs. Bunjee, her whiskers bristling, put her paws on her hips. "That's about enough out of *you*, Miss Bummy, or whatever your name is. Our Professor Capybara will get a proper answer from you, or I'm very much mistaken. Buck, you're the biggest—you carry her."

Buck nodded, adjusting the straps on his harness. "All right, Mother. Chippy, Joe—tie the lady on."

"*What?*" Miss Barmy bared her teeth. "This is ridiculous. I am *not* going anywhere on a *chipmunk*. Release me! I demand—"

"Gag her," Buck ordered.

"Yes, *sir*." The Rat snapped into a perfect Cub Scout salute, and tightened the shoelace around her mouth again.

"Mmpff! Rmmff!" came from Miss Barmy.

Emmy stroked the Endear Mouse between the ears, calming herself by an act of will. She had to think. If Miss Barmy refused to tell where the Extract of Gerbil was, then perhaps—yes—perhaps there *was* another way.

"Chippy," said Buck, "you carry Emmy. Mother, can you manage Joe?"

"Of course," Mrs. Bunjee answered, already pulling another harness from a little pack and tossing it to Chippy. "I'm not feeble yet."

Emmy patted the Endear Mouse on the back, urging it forward. "Can you take a little more weight, Buck?"

Buck shrugged. "Sure. Endear doesn't weigh much more than a dandelion anyway."

Miss Barmy, trussed like a turkey, strained against the shoelace, her eyes furious above the gag. The Endear Mouse perched behind her, gripping her waist tightly.

But the mouse's eyes grew troubled. It let go of Miss Barmy's waist and inched backward.

Emmy shook her head. "Hang on to her, Endear. It won't be for long." She got on Chippy's back and strapped herself in.

Buck stood on his hind legs. "Buckle up, kids— here we go!"

Chippy bounded up—chair, desk, windowsill— and Emmy's head jerked back with the sudden motion as they vaulted through the air. Shaken, she gripped the harness more tightly.

"All right back there?" Chippy spoke over his shoulder.

Emmy looked over the ledge. It was a *long* way down.

"We're all right." Joe, a little breathless, leaned over Mrs. Bunjee's back. "Just think of it as a roller coaster, Emmy."

"Whooaaa!" The cry was torn out of her mouth as Chippy sprang off the window ledge into thin air. Emmy's throat clenched as she looked down at the lawn far below and the oak leaves on branches that looked impossible to reach.

Chippy scrabbled with his claws and barely gripped the tip of a branch. It bent under the sudden weight, and Emmy swung upside down.

Blue sky—hot sun—leaves with thick veins waved overhead, and a green caterpillar as thick as her arm paused in its munching to stare at them. Then they were right-side up again, and safe on the sturdy part of the branch. Emmy started breathing again.

"Whew!" Chippy wiped his forehead with his paw. "I forgot to calculate for the extra weight!"

"Careful," warned Buck, from the next branch over. "That was a near thing."

"Too true," said Chippy. "All right, you rats?"

"All—right—" wheezed Raston, gripping a branch for dear life. Sissy nodded rapidly several times, her eyes tightly shut.

"All right, then—onward!" said Chippy, and leaped again.

Oh, help, Emmy thought as she felt Chippy's hind legs bunch. And then they launched into the air—rising, falling, landing with a bump—another spring, another heart-stopping landing, another jump.

Miss Barmy flew past, clinging desperately to Buck's harness, her chin dropped in a soundless shriek. Emmy laughed, suddenly exhilarated. Up, down, leap and land—now that she was used to it, riding on Chippy's back *was* like a thrilling roller coaster that went on and on. She loved the rushing wind through her hair, and the soaring feeling at the top of each leap, and the green smell of the leaves as they brushed by her face. It might be fun to be a chipmunk.

A last, rolling leap. A dizzying scamper headfirst down a tree. A rush across a lane to the front door of the Antique Rat—a scratching at the door—and they were in.

"Well, well, who have we here?" The professor, kneeling on the floor, untied Miss Barmy from Buck's back. The Endear Mouse jumped away with a look of relief and ran to Emmy's arms.

"Bad—bad lady—bad—" came the thought, like a whimper in Emmy's mind.

Emmy held the little mouse close and thought a certain thought with all her strength.

The Endear Mouse twisted in her embrace and looked up, its eyes bright and alert. It sent another thought back—and Emmy laughed aloud.

"Is that all of it?" she asked.

The Endear Mouse nodded happily.

"Good," said Emmy. She moved to the still trussed Miss Barmy, slid a hand into the nanny's left-side pocket, and pulled out a little vial. Brian's lettering was still visible on the tiny label.

"Mmmmmff!"

Emmy ignored the nanny. "Here's your Extract of Gerbil," she said, holding it out to the professor. "It shrunk some, I guess—but it's all there."

Professor Capybara nodded with deep satisfaction and tucked it safely away. "I am so *very* relieved, my dear," he said, setting Emmy and Joe on the desktop.

The rodents swarmed up the desk legs. Brian, who had been in the back room, shouldered through the velvet curtain holding a cage. And the professor picked Miss Barmy up by the shoelace ends and began to cut her bonds with nail scissors.

"Now really, Miss Barmy," he said, setting her on the desk blotter, "you mustn't play around with rodent powers like this. Just see how you've shrunk yourself!"

"It's not *my* fault," she said icily. "I know these rodents have unusual powers—but I never dreamed that Emmaline would use them against *me*."

The nanny fished a tiny mirror out of her pocket and made an attempt to smooth her hair, tangled from the wild ride through the treetops. "You may not be aware of it, Professor, but Emmaline has severe mental problems, well documented by the school psychologist. They have an opening for her at the Home for Troubled Girls. You've heard of it, I'm sure?"

The professor looked at her with distaste. Brian set Cheswick's cage on the desk with a clank.

"Jane!" Cheswick Vole's voice squeaked as he caught sight of Miss Barmy, and he rattled the bars of his cage. "Oh, Jane, my precious, we're the same size now. Think how happy we could be together."

"Stop blathering," snapped Miss Barmy, "and tell me how to get bigger!"

"She's the one," said Cheswick, pointing at Sissy as Brian set his cage on top of the desk. "She gives you a kiss, and then you grow."

"I should have known it would be something disgusting." Miss Barmy looked at Sissy coldly. "Very well, then, hurry up, can't you? And don't slobber when you do it."

Sissy looked at her doubtfully. "But I don't *want* to kiss you."

Miss Barmy reared back. "Professor," she hissed angrily, "make her do it!"

Professor Capybara leaned back in his chair. "I'm very much afraid," he said to the ceiling, "that I do not have the right to *make* her do anything."

Miss Barmy laughed coldly. "I've made people do what I want all my life, and it never bothered *me*." She advanced on Sissy, her hands grasping. "Kiss me, you wretched rodent! Kiss me, or you'll regret it—"

She grabbed Sissy around the throat. The professor sat up in his chair with a bang, but the Rat was quicker. He leaped forward, snarling.

Miss Barmy twisted beneath him. "Let go," she screamed, clawing at his face—"*Aaiiiiigh!*"

Mrs. Bunjee gasped.

"Already shrunken, and bitten again," said the professor, the joy of research lighting his eyes. "I've always wanted to watch what happens. Haven't you, Raston?"

25

Miss barmy looked ghastly. Her face twitched— shifted—twitched again—

"She's turning into a *rat*!" cried Cheswick. "Oh, my darling Barmy, *stop*!"

It was true. The transformation happened as they watched. Small pink ears grew triangular and large. Eyes grew beady and black. Miss Barmy's carefully coiffed hair flattened, grew furry, and extended down her body in patches of brown and white and tan. Her elegant face narrowed, lengthened, and grew whiskers on either side of a pink, twitching nose. Last of all came the tail. Miss Barmy turned, trying to see what was happening to her, caught sight of it, and fainted dead away.

There was a stunned silence.

"She's kind of cute like that," said Raston at last. "Those little feet in the air and all."

"I like her this way best," said Joe cheerfully. "Completely silent."

There was a sound of sobbing from the cage. "Oh, my Barmsie," sniveled Cheswick. "Oh, Janie, darling, my sweetheart . . ."

The professor rubbed his hands together. "Fascinating. Simply *fascinating*. The way her hands changed to paws! And that little twitching nose!" He reached for a pad of paper and began to make notes.

"But Maxwell," quavered Cheswick, "surely you aren't going to leave her that way?"

"I suppose we can't," said the professor absently, still writing. "Cecilia, would you kiss her now, please?"

Emmy looked from Sissy to the professor. "So Sissy's kiss will turn her back from a rat to a human?"

"Yes, yes, it should. Cecilia and Raston each counteract the effects of the other." Professor Capybara set down his pen and looked up.

Miss Barmy—or the rat that had been Miss Barmy—stirred, sat up, and smoothed her paws over her stomach. She looked down at her brown and white patches and gave a little shriek. "Good heavens, I'm a piebald!"

"That's not so bad," said Sissy. "At least you don't have red eyes."

322

"Well? Kiss me!" Miss Barmy demanded. "I certainly can't spend the rest of my life as a *rat*."

"That's for sure," said Raston. "You'd be a disgrace to the species."

Sissy grimaced, kissed Miss Barmy's whiskered cheek, and stepped back to watch the transformation.

The clock on the wall ticked loudly in the waiting silence.

"Does it . . . usually take this long?" Miss Barmy asked, looking at her paws.

The professor stroked his beard thoughtfully.

"Kiss me again," commanded the brown and white rat.

Professor Capybara's eyes never left the piebald rat as Cecilia kissed her again—and again. And then Miss Barmy began to wail—high, frightened squeaks that ran along Emmy's nerves like the screech of scraping tin.

"Shut her up, I can't think," said the professor irritably.

Raston, Buck, and Chippy surrounded the rat that had been Miss Barmy and gagged her firmly.

"Does the power wear off when it's overused?" Professor Capybara muttered. "There's something

323

here I don't understand. Why doesn't Cecilia's kiss have any effect?"

"I know why." The thought was inside Emmy's head—but it was not her own thought. She looked down at the Endear Mouse, who was pressed against her side.

"Wait," said Emmy. "The Endear Mouse knows."

The professor looked up, startled.

"Why, Endear?" Emmy asked. "Tell me."

The Endear Mouse laid its paw in her hand and looked around the circle.

"She can't turn around," Emmy said, repeating the words that came to her.

"What?"

"What does that mean?"

"How does the mouse know?"

Voices mingled in confusion. The professor raised a hand for quiet.

"The Endear Mouse can read thoughts when it touches someone," Emmy explained. "It held on to Miss Barmy the whole way here. That's how I knew where to look for the Gerbil Extract."

Miss Barmy's thin rat lips curled.

"But 'can't turn around'? What does that mean, I wonder?" the professor murmured.

No one spoke. Emmy quietly held the mouse's paw.

"Okay," she said at last, looking at the faces above her. "I think I've got it. The Endear Mouse doesn't really understand how it all works—"

"None of us completely understand," interrupted Professor Capybara.

"—but it's kind of like there's only one direction Miss Barmy goes. She can get smaller and rattier, all right, but when she's got to become more human, and grow . . ."

Everyone turned to look at the piebald rat. Miss Barmy was grooming herself, looking unconcerned.

The professor nodded slowly. "I see. It's like a two-way street, with something blocking one lane. The traffic can only go south, never north."

Sissy cocked her head. "So what does that mean? Some pathway inside her is all clogged up and won't let my kisses work?"

"Maybe it's all those wormballs," said Joe. "That would clog up anything."

325

"Joe may be right," said the professor, glancing at the charascope. "An undissolved mass of resentment and hate might well have the effect of blocking any kind of growth."

"So Miss Barmy stays a rat?" Joe asked. "For good?"

"There is always the hope that she will change back," said the professor. "But it is likely to be a long and painful process."

"What? Dissolving the hate?" said Emmy.

"And learning to love," said the professor.

A howl broke from Cheswick, and he pounded the bars of his cage. "Let me out!" he cried. "*I* can give her love! *I* can turn her around!"

Miss Barmy rolled her ratty eyes above her gag.

"You can try," said the professor, releasing the latch. "But I suspect it will take more than your efforts alone."

"Dearest Jane," said Cheswick, sliding to his knees, "I've loved you ever since fifth grade, when you let me cheat for you."

Joe snorted.

Cheswick, busy untying Miss Barmy's gag, went on. "And in high school, you were my beauty queen.

I helped count the votes, remember? I made sure you won." He pulled off the gag with a flourish.

"*What?*" Miss Barmy's furry face was outraged. "Did someone get more votes than *me?*"

"Well, yes—your cousin Priscilla. But you *deserved* to win, you were the prettiest."

Miss Barmy preened.

Brian shrugged. "Good looks aren't everything."

"They're practically *nothing*," said the professor briskly.

Cheswick ignored them. "And you *should* have gotten old William's money and the house on the lake. I wanted to help you, so you would know how much I truly cared!"

Cheswick kissed Miss Barmy's hairy paw and continued all the way up to her shoulder. "Oh, my precious tulip, I looooove you," he sang. "Your hair, like the softest silk—"

"Her hair isn't like silk anymore," Joe reminded him.

"Your furry pelt, so brown and white and tan . . ."

"*This* is going to take a while," muttered Chippy.

"Try kissing her again!" said Cheswick, his pale face alight with hope. "She's got to be full of love *now!*"

"I sure hope this is the last time," said Sissy, and she kissed the brown and white cheek.

They all looked at Miss Barmy. If anything, she seemed to look even rattier.

"I'm afraid, Cheswick," said the professor, taking out his pipe, "that your love is not what's required. Jane Barmy *herself* must learn to love."

"Then let me be a rat, too!" cried Cheswick, clasping his hands. "Do this for me, Maxwell. If my love must be a rodent, then shall I be anything but a rat?"

The professor looked at him. "What about the shop?"

"The shop was only a way for me to get close to Jane," Cheswick said desperately. "If I have Jane Barmy herself, why would I need the shop? You can have it. Here—I'll even put it in writing."

The professor lit his pipe, puffing till he had it going steadily. "And what about Brian?"

"Who?" Cheswick looked momentarily confused. "Oh, him."

"Yes, him," said Professor Capybara sternly. "Your nephew."

"He's not really my nephew," said Cheswick Vole. "I just told them that at the orphanage. Cheap labor, you know. You can get rid of him, if you like."

Brian looked stricken to the bone.

The professor flung an arm over Brian's shoulders. "This is a fine young man," he said, "with a big, generous heart. I would be proud to call him my nephew; I only wish he were! He will have a job and a place here for as long as he wants."

Brian's kind, homely face brightened. He looked at the professor with gratitude.

"Come on," said Cheswick, speaking directly to Raston. "Do it. Just a little bite, though—you don't have to take my arm off."

Raston looked at the professor.

Professor Capybara took the pipe out of his mouth. "All right," he said quietly. "If you're *sure*."

Cheswick held out his arm and shut his eyes. The Rat nipped it lightly.

As a man, Emmy thought as she watched the transformation, Cheswick Vole had looked rather ratty. But as a rat, he was undeniably handsome. His eyes were dark and bold, his muzzle well whiskered, and his coat was a glossy black.

Buck untied the gag from around Miss Barmy's furry head. She sat up on her haunches, trotted over to Cheswick, and sniffed.

"Not bad," she said grudgingly. "But listen up, Cheswick. I'm not living in Rodent City with a bunch of chipmunks."

"You haven't been invited," said Mrs. Bunjee stiffly.

"Chessie." Miss Barmy leaned her head next to his and showed her buckteeth. "I know some people across the way. They'd be glad to take us in."

"All right," said Cheswick, looking dazed but elated. "Anything you want, my little rosebud, my precious, my Janie Wanie—"

"Can it," said Miss Barmy succinctly and swarmed down the desk leg. Cheswick followed, seemingly enjoying his newfound agility.

"Watch out for cats," said the professor genially, holding the door open.

"Ah, go kiss a duck," said Miss Barmy as she skittered off.

They all looked out the window as the two rodents scampered over the green. A white curtain fluttered at an upstairs window across the way, followed by a terra-cotta blur and a sudden crash.

"I HATE rodents!" The screech carried clearly through the still summer air.

"Mrs. Bee," Joe said.

"Mother! NO!" came a thin cry from the ground.

Emmy looked at Joe, realization dawning. It wasn't Mrs. Bee, like the insect—it was Mrs. B., for Barmy! And Mr. B. was Jane Barmy's father, who must have taught her to whittle!

"No wonder she's the way she is," said Joe, "with a mother like that."

Emmy nodded in instant agreement. But the professor shook his head.

"Jane Barmy had two parents," he said, puffing away as he stared out the window. "She had a loving example before her, as well as a vicious one. She made her choice."

The professor pointed with the stem of his pipe. "Looks like Cheswick and Miss Barmy made it across, and perhaps even into a tunnel. They'll be fine. But now—"

"Now we set the rodents in the back room free?" asked Brian.

The professor put a hand on Brian's shoulder. "Not yet, son. No, we have another task first. Joe, Emmy, it's time for you to grow."

"Yes, Monica, it's quite a story." Studley Jackell flashed his teeth for the camera. "Joe Benson has been found, but questions about his disappearance still remain. Where is Cheswick Vole, the prime suspect in the case? And what is his connection to Miss Jane Barmy, nanny for the Addison family, who is now under investigation by the police?"

A photo of Miss Barmy flashed on the TV screen at the police station. Emmy and Joe, side by side in a waiting room, watched with rapt attention as they munched on pizza that Officer Carl had brought.

"What indeed, Studley. I understand that a classmate of Joe Benson's, young Emmy Addison, was also at risk?"

"That's right, Monica. On a tip from Professor Maxwell Capybara, police arrived at the Addison home to find lawyers drawing up papers that would give their nanny, Miss Jane Barmy, complete control—"

Emmy shuddered. It had been a narrow escape. But Professor Capybara had things well in hand. Once they were back to full size, he had called the police. And he seemed to know just what to say.

"But what should we tell them?" Emmy had asked as he hung up the phone. "They'll have all kinds of questions!"

The professor had chuckled as he took out his pipe. "Why, if I were you, I'd tell them the truth," he said. "That's always best, don't you think?"

The police had come at once. The professor had gone to talk to Emmy's and Joe's parents himself. And now the toughest decision Emmy had to make was whether she wanted pepperoni or sausage.

"And so police are continuing to search for partners in crime Jane Barmy and Cheswick Vole," intoned the voice of Studley Jackell, as photos of Cheswick and Jane appeared again.

"They look furrier now," muttered Joe through a mouthful of crust.

"A truly amazing story, Studley. But even more amazing is the personal service you get at Ron Ronson's Used Cars . . ."

Officer Carl, the policeman who had picked them up, came into the room and rubbed his mustache. "Okay, you kids. I want you to repeat what you told me to Sergeant Harrison here. You know, about the rats."

Joe put down his pizza, and swallowed. "There were these rats, see, and they shrank Emmy and me—," he began.

"And we went for rides on the chipmunks," added Emmy, wiping her mouth with a napkin.

"They play a great game of pawball," Joe said with enthusiasm. "Only we had to duck into gopher holes when the cats came—"

"They have a whole city underground, with electricity and everything—"

"And we fought Muffy with a cocklebur catapult!"

Officer Carl cleared his throat. "Do you see what I mean, sir? They're just talking crazy."

Sergeant Harrison shook his head. "The suspect must have drugged them," he said gloomily, running a finger around the inside of his collar. "Hallucinogens, most likely. Probably out of their system by now, but the memories linger."

"Yes, sir." Officer Carl pulled down his jacket and

looked sternly at the children. "You'll see your parents soon. In the meantime, try to stop thinking about those rats and all. It's not healthy."

"Emmy, Joe," said the professor, walking in through the open door. "Your parents are here to take you home."

"Cool!" cried Joe, running out of the room. "See you guys later!"

Emmy stood still. "Professor . . . my parents . . ."

"They're back to normal, Emmy." Professor Capybara's eyes twinkled behind his half-glasses. "Well, more or less."

"What do you mean? Did the chinchilla imprint really wear off this soon?"

"Mmm, not exactly. I helped the process along with a little accelerant in their coffee." He looked sheepish. "I didn't remember how it worked until I found it in my notes this afternoon. It was right there all the time—Essence of Hamster."

Emmy frowned. "What does it do?"

"It just speeds things up a bit. It won't work with anything permanent, you understand—not the Snoozer virus, alas—but with temporary conditions it has quite a good effect. Miss Barmy may have even used it on you, when she was impatient for results." He grinned, raising his bushy eyebrows. "It just has one unfortunate side effect, but that should wear off in, oh, about a week."

"Side effect?" said Emmy. "What side effect?"

"It's harmless," said the professor, "but just the teensiest bit startling."

"Emmy!" cried her parents, as they swept through the door and gathered her into their arms. "You're safe!"

Emmy leaned back from their embrace and started to laugh.

Their faces were bright orange.

26

THE SKY WAS A VIVID, clear blue, with small white clouds drifting slowly across Emmy's field of vision. The lake made little lapping sounds at the edge of the sand, and Emmy, flat on her back, was filled with a quiet gladness that almost seemed too big to express.

Just yesterday, Miss Barmy had almost succeeded in her plans. But she hadn't.

Instead, this morning, the Addisons had gone to church together. They had had a picnic lunch on the shore. And now Emmy's mother was lounging in the hammock, reading, and Emmy's father was busy getting the boat ready to sail.

So what if their faces were still orange? It would wear off. Emmy's face had gone back to normal the time Miss Barmy had used the same stuff on her.

Emmy wandered into the house and stopped in front of the picture of the old man in his pinstriped suit. William Addison still looked sad, but now she knew why. His wife and daughter had died, and he had been stuck with Miss Barmy.

"You poor thing," Emmy said to his portrait, wishing she could have given him something to make him feel loved—a hug, or maybe just a plate of cookies. . . .

And then all at once she remembered.

She *had* seen him before—in her parents' bookstore, in raggedy clothes, sitting and talking about books with her father, smiling as her mother brought out a plate of cookies, warm from the oven.

He had never told them his name was William Addison, or that he was rich, and a distant relative. He had come in disguise, to see what kind of people they were. And he had found out.

A feeling of pity welled up in Emmy. Poor, clueless Miss Barmy—she hadn't needed to use Lemming Drops and Prairie Dog Pus and who knew what else to get old William to leave her everything. All he had been looking for was friendship and a little kindness.

There was a rustling sense of expectation in the audience.

The old-fashioned casement windows of the Antique Rat had been washed until every pane sparkled. The cages had been moved from the back room to the front and were stacked among the carved and painted antiques.

On a gilded table near the door were refreshments—little iced cakes, smooth round mints, baskets of nuts—and Brian, with a new haircut, was mixing the punch. The Rat, with a crumpled paper gripped in his paw, paced anxiously back and forth on the desktop.

"We haven't practiced enough . . . and the tenors still miss their cue. . . ."

"Don't worry, Rasty," said Cecilia, patting his paw. "You're going to be *wonderful*." She smiled at the nervous-looking rodents grouped by the desk lamp, every one of which was wearing a big red bow. "You're all going to be wonderful; I just know it."

Emmy, seated on a blue velvet sofa and surrounded by her friends, clapped enthusiastically as Professor Capybara stood up.

"Dear friends and rodents," said Professor Capybara, smiling as he looked around, "we are gathered here today to right an old wrong, and release those who should never have been kept captive. Brian, the first combination, please."

Brian consulted a list in his hand and dialed a series of numbers on a cage whose sign read "Australian Water Rat." A jaunty-looking rat wearing a blue neckerchief stepped out and took a bow to enthusiastic applause.

"The Beaver."

Brian dialed a second combination, and the beaver ambled through the door of its cage, flashing bright orange teeth in a happy grin.

"The Chinchilla. The Chinese Pygmy Dormouse."

Emmy leaned back as the list of names went on. She was looking forward to the next few weeks, when she could finally make some friends at school. And summer was coming, too. Maybe she and Joe could learn to sail.

"The Flying Squirrel," the professor went on. "The Giant Rat of Sumatra."

An exceptionally large and sullen-looking rat lumbered out of its cage and went immediately under the couch, out of the spotlight.

"The Jerboa."

"The Kangaroo Rat."

A small, very hoppy rodent came bounding out of its cage, leaped up onto Emmy's sofa, and sat attentively with its feet straight out in front. After a while it looked shyly at the Endear Mouse.

The Endear Mouse hid its face with its paws.

"Oh, go on and play." Emmy, amused, gave it a gentle nudge with her mind.

"The Prairie Dog," announced Professor Capybara, flipping a page. "The Red Squirrel. The Spiny Pocket Mouse."

They were almost through the alphabet. Emmy looked at the freed rodents, all sitting in the audience now. Every one of them wore a look of exhilaration. Every one of them seemed to be breathing a little deeper, a little more freely.

"The Striped Gopher. The Syrian Hamster."

"Almost time for refreshments," whispered Joe.

Emmy shook her head. "Not yet. Look at Raston."

The Rat was as nervous as Emmy had ever seen him. Gnawing on a pencil, feverishly making small notes on a torn piece of paper, his mouth moved as if he was saying words over to himself, while his tail twitched spasmodically. Behind him, the little group of rodents looked frozen in place.

"Performance anxiety," whispered Emmy, knowing the symptoms.

"The Tree Porcupine. And—the Woodland Jumping Mouse."

There was sustained applause. The rodents embraced one another, wiping away tears. The Kangaroo Rat and the Endear Mouse, holding paws, hopped up and down on the sofa.

"But, Professor," said the deep voice of the muskrat. "What do we do now? Where should we go?"

"An excellent question," said Professor Capybara, beaming as if a particularly bright student had just spoken up in class, "and one you should all consider carefully. First, I will not abandon you. You may stay here at the Antique Rat for as long as you need to make up your mind."

Mrs. Bunjee stood up on her chair. "Some of you smaller rodents may want to consider living in Rodent City."

"We can always use burrowers," added Chippy. "We're enlarging our tunnel system every year."

Buck cleared his throat. "If you prefer country living, there's waterfront property along Grayson Lake and the creeks thereabouts. Just watch out for the wild rodents. They speak a primitive dialect, and they like to throw nuts."

A golden hamster stood on its hind legs. "Can I go back home to Syria?"

"And wh-what about the ocean?" stuttered an excitable salt marsh mouse.

The professor spread out his hands. "If you want to go back to your native land, talk to me. In the meantime, though, if any of you would be willing to assist me in my research, I would very much appreciate it."

There was a dead silence.

"What do you mean?" said the surly voice of the Giant Rat of Sumatra. "You plannin' to tie us down, an' lock us up, an' stick needles in us?"

The professor shook his head. "Not at all. I will never force you. But I would like to discover more about you rodents. Every one of you has a very special power; one that can be used to help, or to harm. To hold someone hostage, or to set them free . . ."

Raston moved to the center of the desk, clutching his sweat-stained piece of paper.

"We can discuss that later on, however. Now," said Professor Capybara, "we conclude with a rodent version of 'America the Beautiful,' written and conducted by our very own Raston Rat!"

There was a sudden hush. The Rat lifted a shaking paw.

Sissy smiled at him proudly.

Raston's shoulders straightened. He threw back his head. "Hmmm," he began, giving the note. And then, in four-part harmony, the rodent chorus sang:

> Oh, pitiful, the pellets dry
> And the wood shavings damp
> Rats running round in metal wheels
> Until their hind legs cramp . . .
> But captive rats can boldly dream
> Till prisoned rats are free
> Till, as they should, in rodenthood
> They squeak in liberty!
>
> Oh, beautiful, for freedom sweet
> For cages open wide,
> For furry rodents' scampering feet
> Throughout the countryside . . .
> Oh rodent cities, rodent fields
> Oh rodent country grand—
> May noble rodents ever fill
> This happy, ratty land!

There was utter silence as the last note faded away. The Rat looked around, uncertain. "I . . . I had a third verse," he said apologetically, "but the last line wouldn't scan. . . ."

The silence lingered a moment more. Mrs. Bunjee sniffled and blew her nose. And then the room exploded with whistles, paw stomping, and thunderous applause. The rodent choir began to cheer, too.

"Take a bow, Ratty," said Emmy, prodding him.

Small eyes shining, the Rat grabbed for Sissy's paw. "I could never have done it without you," he whispered, and they bowed together as the applause went on and on.

Emmy and Joe made their way to the refreshment table and stood by the open door, eating. The air was warm and fresh, and the little iced cakes were delicious. Outside, on the green, a white puppy ran, barking happily.

Joe nudged Emmy. "Look who showed up," he murmured.

Perched on the windowsill, looking in, were two rats—one piebald, one glossy black.

"Have a mint, my precious tulip?" offered the black rat gallantly.

Miss Barmy crammed the mint into her mouth

and chewed, her furry cheeks distended. "That professor's a fool," she said indistinctly. "Those rats were worth *millions*."

"What do I care, my dainty cupcake?" said Cheswick Rat, nuzzling her. "I have you . . . that's all any rat could want."

The piebald rat stiffened. "Get your nose off my ear this *instant*," she said frostily.

"Oh, come now, my little chicken dumpling."

"I'll chicken dumpling you, you old fool!" screeched Miss Barmy, unsheathing her claws.

With a yelp, Cheswick Rat leaped off the windowsill and took off across the grass. Miss Barmy, her claws outstretched, was close behind.

Emmy and Joe watched them scuttle across the green, their tails in the air.

"She wasn't much of a nanny," said Joe thoughtfully. "Or even a decent human being. But you've got to admit, Emmy . . ."

"What?"

Joe grinned. "She makes an excellent rat."